ROBERT ARCHER PARANORMAL MYSTERIES

NOVELLA COLLECTION

ASHLEY GARDNER

JA / AG PUBLISHING

CONTENTS

A MATTER OF HONOR

A ROBERT ARCHER PARANORMAL MYSTERY NOVELLA

CHAPTER ONE

London, 1820

Y ou are a drunken lout," my brother, Sir Frederick Archer, shouted at me in his fog-gloomed sitting room in Berkeley Square the Michaelmas after the *drohner* had disappeared. "Gin-soaked and pox-brained. What luck that Bonaparte has been defeated at last—I wager the King's army would not take you now."

"I do not have the pox," I said with dignity. Alas, my words slurred, because I was, as accused, gin-soaked.

Margery, his wife, cringed in a chair by the window, pretending interest in her needlework. She had the complexion of a tallow candle, her hair a golden color those with very fair hair in youth sometimes acquired.

I, Robert Archer, the younger brother, had paid a call on her, my dear sister-in-law, to ask if she could spare a few shillings until my next pay packet. But my brother had come upon us before I was able to make my request and had taken the opportunity to lecture.

When he paused for breath, I said, "You are angry, and blame me for losing the *drohner*. I did not steal the bloody thing." But I'd had it in my care when it had vanished three months ago, and that thought haunted me every moment of every day. The *drohner* was shared between family members, passing from house to house. It had been in mine when it went missing.

"You *displayed* it," Frederick snapped. "In your front room to your drunken friends—dear God. You broke a sacred family trust."

"It is not unique." I made the excuse I'd been making since the thing had gone. "My friends had seen one before —every gentleman's family has one. None are secret, for all they're locked away like the crown jewels." The speech taxed my sodden brain, and I dropped to the nearest chair, my legs too shaky to hold me.

"Even the king has one, Frederick," Margery said timidly.

My brother swung on his wife, dark eyes ablaze. "What he has is false, created on a pretense to make his family seem more connected to English ones. Ours had the lines, the power, the magic of our ancestors for seven hundred years. Now gone. Because of *his* carelessness."

He thrust a finger at me. Behind him, Margery gave me a helpless look from her light brown eyes, which I returned. We both writhed under my brother's thumb. Frederick had been a strong, muscular man—now he was running to fat, his face round and red, his brown hair lank. I'd look like him before long unless I had a care. At the same time his waistcoat and frock coat hung in loose folds on him as though he'd lost weight since the *drohner* had gone, his breeches wrinkled about his knees.

"And he has made no effort to retrieve it," Frederick carried on. "Three months since it has gone, and he has done *nothing*. He is not fit to belong to our family. I do not even know why you are here, Robert."

I did not tell him I'd come for money. Margery had enough misery without her husband knowing she occasionally let me touch her for blunt.

I pried myself out of the chair, said polite good-byes to Margery, and escaped the house. But I had left empty-handed.

I'd have to sell my commission, I reflected as I walked along the rain-soaked pavement of Berkeley Square. Night had fallen, and the golden smudge of gaslights behind the fog did little to light the way.

I had hung onto my commission in part to annoy my brother but mostly because it meant something to me. A lieutenant's pay did not carry far, and my father had left me nothing. My brother had inherited everything—the baronetcy, land, money, houses—but my father hadn't felt any obligation to provide for his younger son. I had nothing but my pay packet, meager as it was, and my rank, my own form of honor.

But my brother was wrong. I had been searching for the *drohner*. I cared as much for it as did Frederick, and I bled with guilt. Frederick was right—I should have looked after the bloody thing better.

A *drohner*, in its most basic sense, is a square of polished black stone, pretty to look upon, but it is much more than that. Every *drohner* holds its family's power.

Every son puts his hand on his family's *drohner* the day of his majority and swears to protect it. Every dying man holds it between his hands, giving to it his magics to carry to the next generation. The *drohner* was kept in a place of pride in the household, hidden from all eyes but the family's, and its magic protected the family and gave it honor.

Other families, old and powerful ones, had lost *drohners* or had seen them destroyed by their enemies. Those families had dwindled, faded into nothingness. I wondered how much time would pass before our family suffered the same fate.

Margery, in her ten-year marriage to Frederick, had been brought to bed of one child, stillborn, and had borne no more. Frederick made her feel it keenly. And I, unmarried, childless—as far as I knew—stumbled through the streets of London without tuppence in my pocket.

Which is why the attack surprised me when it came. Why should ruffians bother to rob me?

I heard the swift tramp of feet, then a heavy blow landed on the back of my neck—not a fist, a cosh. My legs buckled and the pavement rose up to knock the wind from me. The owner of a huge boot kicked me in the ribs. Another kick, from a smaller boot but no less painful, landed on the small of my back. A pair of beefy hands shoved my face to the cobbles, and fists pummeled me. Blood spattered from my parted lips as I tried to explain I had no money, no watch, nothing.

Abruptly the boot vanished from my back, the hands from my neck. I took a long breath, blood clogging my nose. I raised my head, but blackness danced before me, and I fell, hard, to the pavement again.

I awoke, facedown in my own bed. My head throbbed, my tongue lay like lead in my mouth.

Another drunken binge, I decided. Then I saw that my hands, which were wrapped in bandages, lay on either side of my head like leprous slugs.

The clink of glass on glass came to me. I turned my head to see, in the light of a lone candle, a slim woman pouring liquid from a decanter into a glass. I prayed it was brandy.

The woman had blond hair, a deeper golden than her high-waisted gown, wound into a heavy braid on the crown of her head. Her eyes were dark, nearly black. Otherwise, she was ordinary, with a face pretty but not extraordinarily so, a trim figure, not heavily buxom. Her dress was cotton, floating lace, clean and mended.

In outward appearance, she looked like a woman I might brush by in the street or see in the markets or at Exeter 'Change. But her eyes, deep and black, the irises swallowing her pupils, betrayed her. I would never in my life forget those haunted eyes I'd seen a few years ago as she'd implored me, from behind a pile of crates, to take her child from her and go.

I forced open my dry lips. *"You."*

She came to me and slipped a long-fingered hand under my head. Alas, the glass held only water. I drank deeply, suddenly burning with thirst.

"You did me a good turn once," she said. "I vowed to do you one, if I could."

Her voice was smooth, still with calm. Quite unlike the terrified tremor it had held that night in Covent Garden.

I'd only been *half*-drunk that night. She'd crouched in

the shadows, blood all over her gown, and she'd thrust the squalling bundle at me. "Please, take her. Take her far away."

I'd stared stupidly at the screwed up face and closed eyes, the pink lips drawn back from gums in a silent cry of hunger.

"Where on earth am I to take her?"

She'd only looked at me as she laid the bundle in my arms, her eyes pools of terror. I'd assumed her a game girl, gotten with child by some flat, hiding in the corner for her lying-in. Her desperation stabbed me so deep that I had to look away to shut it out.

The babe had squirmed, its mouth seeking nourishment in the faded braid of my uniform. When I'd looked back for the young woman, she'd vanished into the shadows, leaving me alone with her child.

I'd taken the babe to a woman called Lizzie in St. Martin's Lane. She'd been a wet nurse and had a healthy brood of her own. Without questioning me, she'd taken the bundle into her competent hands and sent her oldest boy scurrying away to find a girl she knew who'd just birthed. The son returned with the bleary-eyed girl in tow, and soon the tiny life was happily suckling at her bosom.

Lizzie and I had then stolen a few moments together in the cellar while her husband snored on in the kitchen surrounded by the fruit of his loins. From time to time, during the last year or two, I'd followed my curiosity back to the house where the babe still lived, adopted by the large-hearted Lizzie into her own ample family.

I finished the water, and she lowered me down on my

stomach again. I'd been far too tired to turn over, even to drink.

"Did you bring me home by yourself?" I croaked at her. I hardly thought it likely. She looked much better than when I'd last seen her, her cheeks pale but not deathly so, her gown whole and unstained, her movements competent and easy. Robust, yes, but not robust enough to carry me here without help.

She set the empty glass on my bedside table. "I did, yes."

I looked at her slim arms and tried to smile. "You couldn't drag a cat home, miss, let alone a drunken lieutenant no better than he ought to be."

Her hand landed with a suddenness on my neck, and she pinned me to the bed with hideous strength. My face smashed into the ticking and I could not draw breath.

"Had you not guessed?" she asked.

Watery fear washed my bones. I struggled against the pressure on my neck, which was no more use than struggling against an oak tree. Once on a battlefield in Portugal, a French soldier had risen from the scrub not three feet from me and pointed his pistol at my forehead. I'd stared into that round, black barrel of oblivion and smelled death.

Upon firing, the pistol had kicked faintly to the left, and the ball had whizzed by my ear. The French soldier had cursed mightily then died with my sergeant's bayonet in his stomach.

That fear was nothing to what I felt now.

She was a night-slayer. They crawled London's seedy darkness late at night, feeding on the blood of the helpless, the lone wayfarer, those who had nowhere to turn. They took the old, the young, the healthy, the sick, all without discrimination. They'd infested the city from time to time in the past, until the terror-stricken citizenry had demanded they be rooted out. The last infestation had been in 1750, when a pack had descended into St. Giles and ruled there until the King's army had been sent to drive them away. There had been no infestation since then—nearly seventy years ago now—though reports from time to time of night-slayer-like killings had led to panic and every Bow Street Runner brought in to hunt the slayer.

Night-slayers did not die, except from starvation. They shunned the light, but it did not harm them. They were vermin, skulking in the night and shadows like rats, but they could also look like ordinary people—a game girl, a beggar, a lamp-lighter, or a blond young woman who'd saved me from robbery tonight.

"Are you going to kill me?" I asked, my voice weak with fear.

She released me so abruptly that I slumped into the ticking, spent and exhausted.

"I could have killed you where you lay in the street," she said. "I did not."

I turned my head to stare at her, then a thought struck me. "God's truth, that child was not a night-slayer, was it?" I had given it to Lizzie and her family—what had I done?

She looked, to my surprise, amused. "Night-slayers are made, not born. She is as alive as you are. Why do you think I begged you to take her away? I did not wish to harm her in my hunger. I still have a heart that feels and grieves." She pinned me with her hard gaze. "Is she safe?"

"Yes. I took her to—"

"I know where you took her. Is she well?"

I nodded into the mattress. "She is. She has seven brothers and sisters and cream and porridge every day. She was walking the last time I saw her."

Tears shone in the dark eyes for a brief instant, but vanished so quickly I might have imagined them. She turned from the bed and started for the door—I realized she was leaving. Just like that, no good-byes, no more conversation.

"Do you have a name?" I called after her.

"No." At the door, she paused, her hand on the handle. "*You* are Robert Sebastian Archer of the 26th Rifles. In number 24, Exeter Street, Covent Garden."

And then she was gone.

I lay on my bed, immobile, my head pounding and my limbs aching. I did not stop shaking for a long time.

CHAPTER TWO

I seldom stayed home after that encounter. I lodged with friends, in brothels, at my club.

I knew what the night-slayer had been telling me when she'd recited my name and house number. She meant that she knew who I was, where I lived, and where I went each day. She'd already known where I'd taken the child, where Lizzie lived. She must have followed me that night, had been following me ever since, skulking in the shadows, watching my every move. I'd heard stories of night-slayers stalking their victims for years, terrifying them, playing with them, making pets of them, all the while killing them slowly.

But months went by, and I did see not my night-slayer again. The months lengthened to a year. Her daughter grew and talked and ran. I could not stop going to visit her. She called me Uncle Robbie. My fears waned with time, and I fell into my old habits of drinking too much, lying too long abed, avoiding doing anything useful, visiting Lizzie when I could, and touching friends and Margery for money.

And I looked for the *drohner.*

I heard of a man in Wales who'd found one, and I made the journey. But it was not ours. Ours would have called to me, responded to the touch of my hand. This one did nothing. It was a dead black lump, drained of its might by decades in the dirt before the young Welshman had chanced across it while he'd been tending sheep and dug it up.

Every rumor, no matter how small, called me on heartbreaking treks across England, once to France, with only gin to comfort me, but to no avail. Someone had stolen our *drohner* and hidden it from us. One day, it would be as dead and drained as the one I'd seen in Wales, and the Archer family would fade to nothing.

One of the men I'd shown the thing to that fateful night was Daniel Almay, a lieutenant of my regiment, who shared my club and most of my life.

"Saw your sister-in-law last evening at Almack's," he said one night as he opened his box of snuff in the club's library and took a hearty pinch. "She looked a bit wan."

"She's ill," I said with some sadness. "She was increasing again this spring, but didn't come up to scratch."

"Good lord. I am sorry."

I shrugged, hiding my anger. When Margery had delivered her second stillborn child two months ago, Frederick had berated her. I'd gone to pay her a well-wishing visit and heard him lash out at her, calling her weak and a poor excuse for a woman.

I'd turned on Frederick and snarled that perhaps it was his seed that was wanting, not the receptacle. He'd struck me full in the face. I'd leapt at him, ready to do battle, but Margery had screamed at me, begging me to leave him alone.

I'd gone. A month had passed and then Margery had visited me in my rooms. She came in a hired hack, bundled in cloak and deep hood, without her maid or footman.

I watched her through bloodshot, aching eyes, a leftover of my night's oblivion of port and brandy and gin as she sat upright on a chair across the room, so very proper was Margery. She apologized for not inviting me to the house while she recovered, and then for Frederick's behavior toward me that day, but I waved it away.

"Don't worry," I said, my voice a rasp. "You needed time to heal, and old Freddy can't help being a right bastard."

Margery twisted her hands, pulling the soft leather gloves from her thin wrists. "Robert, I ... I so want to have a child."

"I know you do."

"I have been thinking on what you said." She studied the gloves, her lashes black against her pale face. "That perhaps it is not my fault that I have failed."

"No *perhaps* about it," I said, trying to sound cheerful. "It is not your fault at all. Do not let my brother wear you down. He is disappointed, and he looks for someone to blame."

She kept her gaze on her hands. "I know Frederick does not mean to be so beastly."

I disagreed. I was of the opinion that Frederick meant every word of his nasty declarations.

"I would do anything, I think, to have a child." Margery finally raised her head and looked at me, and her cheeks went a dull shade of red.

A long moment of silence hung between us. Upstairs, a woman began shouting drunkenly. A male voice rose, coupled with heavy thumps on the floor. Flakes of loose gray paint floated down and rested on my sleeve.

"Margery ..."

She looked away, shamefaced. "I know it is in your best interest to keep me from conceiving."

She meant that if Frederick died childless, I inherited the lot. Land, wealth, the baronetcy, honor. A single child could cut me out of the succession forever.

I didn't give a damn.

"You are my sister-in-law," I said. "That means that as far as the law is concerned, you are my sister. With everything that goes with it." Anytime I had thought to comfort her in the way I'd learned such comfort from Lizzie, the forbidden nature of such a liaison had stopped me. Margery wasn't a bad sort, pretty in her own way, though tired and worn now. She'd been a beauty when Frederick had courted her—I had met her for the first time when I'd been on leave from trying to kill Frenchman on the Peninsula and had envied Freddie. He had everything, and a lovely woman on top of it.

"I know," Margery said, her voice nearly a whisper. "But you are Frederick's brother."

I stared into her unblinking brown eyes. I read shame

there and beneath it, great hope. She trapped me with that pathetic hope.

So I lay with her, my brother's wife, piling sin atop sin. My gentleness surprised her, I guessed by the tensing of her muscles where she expected pain. I sensed her relax when she did not find it.

I went to Lizzie afterward and tried to erase the deed by committing more sin. My heart ached, and I had been ill at ease ever since.

Daniel Almay returned me to the present by saying: "I suppose she's feeling the loss of the *drohner*. You are not looking so fit yourself."

"May we speak on another subject?" I asked stiffly. I declined his offer of snuff, but I would kill for a gin. The club, alas, offered only the gentlemanly liquids of wine, brandy, and port.

"Not yet," Almay said. "I heard of someone else who recently surfaced with a *drohner*. Gregory Folkstone. He boasted it to me, like the bacon-brain he is."

"Folkstone?" I stifled a snort. "His grandfather was a butler."

"My point exactly. What is a butler's family doing with a *drohner*? It either cannot be genuine, or belongs to someone else."

I sat back. "I don't believe him. If his family had owned it all this time, he would have told the tale before now. And if it is mine—stolen—why would whoever had stolen it suddenly hand it over to Folkstone?"

Almay held out his hands as he shrugged. "Who knows? But don't ignore this, Robert. I worry for you."

I sighed. "It would be stupid not to ask him. Do you know where he is tonight?"

Almay barked a laugh. "Unless he's at death's door, he'll be gaming. Losing all that beautiful blunt his grandfather built for posterity."

I thanked Almay for his information, joined him in a brandy, and left him.

Before I went in search of Folkstone, I paid a call on Derek Chase, the second gentleman I'd showed the *drohner* to before it disappeared.

The world regarded Derek as a silly fellow, but the world was wrong. He had a canny sense behind his affable smile that had built a fortune for him in the City. His simple tastes kept him in a pair of rooms off Jermyn Street where he lived in modest style. He greeted me at the door of those rooms with affection.

"Robert Archer, by all that's holy. Haven't seen you in an age. You look wretched."

He made me sit in his parlor while his manservant brought a bowl of brandy, water, and sugar.

"This is killing you, isn't it?" Derek asked, his eyes narrowing in concern. "Do not shake your head at me; you are fading, my dear fellow. I saw your brother the other day. White as a ghost and thin as a lathe. This is what comes from this wretched *drohner* business. Thank God my ancestors weren't titled and pedigreed and felt the need to have a *drohner*. The idea of putting all a dynasty's strength and hope into a hunk of stone is nonsense. If you lose it, you lose everything. You are vulnerable. Look at you."

"But with a *drohner*, we have the strength of giants," I

answered, sincerely believing it. History had proved it—the Archers had been powerful until this disaster. "Someone out there wants to destroy our strength. And when I find that someone, he will answer for it."

I left him after another bowl of brandy to hunt Folkstone. As I popped in and out of every gaming hell in St. James's, a lightskirt attached herself to me. She wore a tight green silk that showed off her pretty ankles, and a large bonnet that hid her face.

"I'm out at pocket tonight, love," I told her. "And on a mad goose chase besides."

She followed me a little while longer, then drifted away. I never discovered Folkstone, but I found comfort in a cellar gin shop—a short way to hell at a penny a glass.

I dragged myself out at a time respectable people were just beginning to stir. The cold dawn light hurt my eyes, and I walked, half-blind, toward the river.

They waited for me at a turning near Charing Cross, two men armed with cudgels and death in their eyes. I fought madly, drawing blood with my knuckles, but they battered me soundly.

I saw my lightskirt out of the corner of my eye. She ran toward one of the thugs, lifted him from me, and slammed him to the pavement. The other stared in stunned surprise, and died with her fingers in his chest.

I rolled to my feet and ran. Or tried to. My legs shook and buckled, and I could not breathe. In considerable pain, I sagged against a wall and watched the night-slayer murder two men. She ripped out their throats and fed on their blood, while I slid to the ground in terror.

She came to me. She'd removed her bonnet from her sun-yellow hair, and her dark eyes held mine.

"Who were they?" she demanded. "Why did they try to kill you?"

"I do not know," I answered, trying to catch my breath.

"You do know." Her green silk was wet with blood, and blood had spilled from her mouth to dry in rivulets on her white throat. "You *know*. Think."

"I was looking high and low for Folkstone. Maybe someone does not want me to find him." I squeezed my eyes shut. "I told Derek." Had he betrayed me? Had he stolen the *drohner*, for whatever reason, and tried to stop me finding it? "Please, God, not Derek."

"Look at me," my night-slayer said.

I tried to turn away, drunk and weeping. She took my face in her strong hand and forced it to her. I gazed into her bloody face and the cold evil in her eyes, and quailed.

"You have not found your *drohner*, have you?" she asked. "You have not looked. You have killed yourself instead."

"What are you talking about?" I said wearily. "I've searched and searched. I've gone all over England—"

Her fingers dug into my jaw. "You have not looked hard enough. Else you would have found it. You have buried yourself because you fear the truth."

I was alone, aching, and sick. *What truth?* "Why are you trying to save me?"

"I told you why."

Because I'd saved her child. I was Androcles to her lion. I'd pulled the thorn from her paw when I'd taken the little girl to Lizzie. I wondered how long my parole would last.

"Your daughter is growing tall," I said. The girl had become dear to me, and the thought of her brought a faint smile to my cracked lips. "Her hair is the color of sunshine."

My night-slayer slid her hand to my aching chest, tracing a gentle curve over my ribs. "You have a good heart, Robert. I feel it, the goodness in you. It beats through your blood and your body. It is why you are dying."

"I don't . . . understand."

She smiled, cruel and animal-like. "Do you fear me?"

"God, yes."

"Good. Fear keeps you alive. Love and goodness will kill you." She leaned closer, her breath touching me. "Let me find the *drohner* for you."

I tried to shake my head "No..."

"I know where it lies, and why it lies there. You gave me a life. Let me give yours back to you."

I had no idea what she was talking about—how could she know? If the *drohner* were so easy to obtain, I'd have found it by now. "You saved me twice already," I pointed out. "Surely our bargain is finished."

The night-slayer gave me a pitying look. "Robert, you believe that the difference between life and death is breathing and not breathing. The battlefield taught you that. But the difference is so much more. I will give you that understanding, if nothing else."

My head ached and throbbed, and I knew I'd never stand up. "You give me riddles."

"Let me teach you the answers to them, then."

I roused my strength and shook off her hand. "No. You can't understand what this is all about. Our bargain is finished—you have no need to come to my aid again."

She dragged me to my feet with a power that terrified me. "Seek not to bargain with a night-slayer, Robert Archer. You will lose."

My night-slayer threw me aside with easy strength and walked away into the darkness.

CHAPTER THREE

After that night I remained stone-cold sober. I took little more than a glass of port or brandy every day and turned my face from gin shops. The haze receded from my world, and I saw with sharp outlines for the first time in years.

I saw that my brother was no more than an idiotic brute who enjoyed tormenting his wife because the law gave him leave to. I saw that I had succumbed to self-pity and self-indulgence not only over losing the *drohner*, but because I was poor, lonely, struggling, and resented the fact that Freddy had inherited everything. I had a long climb to make out of the abandon to which I'd sunk.

And I saw that my brother was dying.

I saw it in his thin hands, the weary look in his eyes, the pale outline of his lips. His walk had slowed, his steps had become clumsy, his hair thin and lank. A wasting disease, some whispered. The absence of the *drohner*'s protective magic, my friends said. The loss of honor, I knew inside myself. He'd never had much honor to begin with—the loss of the collective honor of the family had broken his heart.

I finally ran Folkstone to ground and flattered him into showing me his *drohner*. It was not ours.

He had it enshrined in his front parlor, in a japanned cabinet with a tiny lock. The polished black cube rested on a cushion of velvet, surrounded by junk—pressed flowers, a cork from the first bottle of port he'd drunk at Carleton House, a diamond stud given him by a lady.

Folkstone did not understand the *drohner* in the least. It was not some memento, to be shut in a curio cabinet until shown to any who asked. Folkstone beamed over his treasure, but I knew it for what it was, an imitation that some artist had made for him, probably for a ridiculous price. A pretty thing, but it did not have the depth, the resonance of old magics beating from the ancient past. I politely admired it, hiding my disgust.

A few months passed. I mulled over what my night-slayer had said, that I knew where our *drohner* was but feared to look for it there. My thoughts darkened and I did not like them. Easier to comb the city, keeping an ear open for any rumors or tales of a stray *drohner* where it did not belong.

My brother slowly sickened, and he would no longer receive me at the house. Margery was belly-full again. I assumed she'd had the intelligence to drag old Frederick off to bed the same night she'd lain with me so that he would not doubt the child was his.

Lizzie's brood grew to include a little boy with hair the same shade of brown as mine. Her good-natured lout of a husband either did not notice or did not care.

On one visit, I told Lizzie I loved her.

"Don't be daft," she whispered as we lay entwined on the blanket in the cellar. "I'm thirty-five if I'm a day."

I traced her cheek. "In all of the world, there is no woman with as good a heart as yours. Whatever happens to me, whatever happens to you—I love you as I love no other."

Lizzie flushed, pleased, and hid her face in my shoulder.

Of the other woman in my life, I saw no sign. I did not forget about her this time, and I had stopped drinking until she receded into the haze. I watched every shadow, every passage, every stray woman who passed me.

But I never saw the night-slayer ... until I went to Lizzie to pay what turned out to be my last visit.

Lizzie's husband was out, and I lingered a little longer than usual. When I put on my clothes and went out to Lizzie's front room, the little girl with sunshine hair came to me.

"Uncle Robbie," she said. "I have your bit of stone."

And she pulled out of her little apron the *drohner*, which had been missing for nearly three years.

CHAPTER FOUR

I stared at it, dumbfounded. The tallow candlelight warmed its polished depths, and its underlying red streaks burned redder as I reached for it.

I felt its magics even before I touched it. I was an Archer, and generations of Archers great and ignoble had poured their magics and their hearts into it. They called to me across the years, and my fingers trembled as I pressed the stone to my own heart.

The *drohner* was smooth to the touch, almost soapy-feeling. It had a heat of its own, which warmed my numb fingers. It sang to me, possessed me, welcomed me home. I closed my eyes, letting the peace of the thing spill over me.

"Robbie, are ye all right?"

I opened my eyes to find Lizzie at my elbow. She smelt of candle grease and lovemaking, and she watched me with tender concern.

"Where did you get it?" I asked the little girl.

"A lady brought it to me. She said you were looking for it."

I stared, alert. "What lady? Who was she?"

"She didn't give no name," the mite said. "She gave it to me and told me you needed it."

I looked at Lizzie in great alarm. "You did not let this woman into your house, did you?"

Lizzie watched me with eyes that held only curiosity. "No, we saw her in the market. She was polite spoken—a lady. Do you know who she was?"

A night-slayer. Whose daughter you've had the keeping of these last four years.

"I must go. I must ... " I trailed off, not certain what I had to do. I absently kissed Lizzie on the cheek. "God bless you, Lizzie," I said and started away.

"Robbie."

Lizzie's voice sounded odd, and I turned back. She was twisting her plump hands in her apron. "Robbie, I think ye should not come back."

I stopped, stricken.

"Don't look at me like that. It's Jack, ye see."

Her husband. I made for her, anger rising. "What has he done? Has he hurt you? Does he know ... ?"

Lizzie's mouth softened into a fond smile. "He's not done a blessed thing. He don't say nothing, but ... He's getting on a bit, Jack is. And he ain't got no one but me."

I stared at her, hurt in my heart and the *drohner* singing in my soul. "You love the lout."

"That I do. I always have."

Yet, she'd spared some little corner of her heart for me. I went to her and touched her cheek. "He's lucky, is Jack."

Lizzie kissed my fingers. "I'll not forget ye, Robbie."

And I would never love another woman as strongly as I loved her. For all Lizzie eked out existence in the back streets of London with eight children and no money, she had more sense than the most sophisticated city trader, more courage than any regimental commander, more compassion, more caring than any gentlewoman I knew.

I kissed her lightly on the lips, my eyes wet. I slid the *drohner* into my pocket, tousled the little girl's sun-colored hair, and left Lizzie's house forever.

———

I SENSED THE NIGHT-SLAYER BEFORE I SAW HER THIS TIME. My sobriety had led me to a heightened state of awareness, so I was not startled when she fell into step beside me in the rainy March darkness as I made my way from Lizzie's street.

I did not ask her where she'd found the *drohner*. I thought I knew, and I feared the knowledge.

"If your brother dies," the night-slayer said in her clear, even voice. "You inherit the lot."

"His son does," I corrected her. "If Margery is carrying a boy and it lives."

"Likely you'd be appointed guardian, as his uncle. You'd have the care of Margery as well. She'd see you would not lose by it."

I stopped in the street. The fog-shrouded darkness was mostly empty—only one person pushed past us, grunting in irritation. "Why do you want Freddy to die?" I asked. "Why should *you* care what happens to me?"

The night-slayer stared at me with fathomless eyes in the face of an ordinary, pretty young woman. "She is a beautiful child. You give your lover money for the keeping of her, don't you?"

"What I can spare, yes. Lizzie and her husband have nothing."

"And you have so little." The night-slayer cocked her head. "Why should you give it, for the child of a creature like me?"

I shrugged, though my chest was tight. "It seems the thing to do."

"You wish to keep her safe, so she will not end up prey for a night-slayer. So that one will not find her and make her like me. You want to give her a chance."

"Yes."

"And for that," she said simply. "I want everything for you." She paused. "What will you do with the *drohner*?"

I had it inside my coat, resting against my chest. "Return it where it belongs."

She studied me a moment, eyes glittering in the dim light. "I will go with you."

"No." Dear God, I did not want her in my brother's house, with Margery ... and my child.

She showed her teeth in a smile. "I will go anyway."

CHAPTER FIVE

My brother's footman gave the night-slayer a disdainful look when we entered the house, clearly not understanding what she was. The night-slayer had dressed respectably enough this evening, but my brother leapt to the same conclusion his servant did.

Frederick entered the small sitting room and bathed us both in his sneer. "What are you doing here, Robert? With one of your doxies, no less?"

I took the *drohner* from my pocket and held it out to him.

Frederick's face drained of color, his mouth dropping open. "Dear God. How did you—"

"Take it."

I set it into his hands. Frederick stared at the *drohner* for one long moment, then he looked up at me, eyes burning in his white face. "You brought it back to me." He whispered. He looked at the black stone with deep reverence. "Do you feel it? It knows it's home. So long. It has been so long . . ."

"Reward him," my night-slayer said sternly to my brother.

Frederick looked up from the *drohner*, blinked. "What?"

"Reward him. For returning it."

Frederick's face regained color, and with it his old obstinacy. "Devil take him. He lost the bloody thing in the first place."

Frederick found himself against the wall with the night-slayer's hand hard on his chest. She brought her face close to his and spoke in slow deliberation.

"You are an empty shell of a man," she said, her voice low and fierce. "Your brother, Robert, keeps his word to a filthy night-slayer who can smell his blood and could kill him in a flash. His honor runs deep within him. *You* believe honor lies in a piece of polished stone. You are a fool."

The night-slayer's fingers split the silk of Frederick's waistcoat and tore into the flesh below. Freddy screamed.

I ran across the room and flung myself on the night-slayer, but my grip could no more move her than I could have moved a stone monolith. "Let him go."

She turned to me, her eyes pools of night. "Without him, you can have everything. His house. His money. His wife. His *life*."

"I don't want them!" I shouted. "I don't want them."

The night-slayer's fingers eased back from Frederick, but only a fraction. "You have nothing. Keep the *drohner*. You can have his riches, his power."

"I don't want it if it makes me like him. The *drohner* is all he has."

The night-slayer regarded me a moment longer, then she wrenched her fingers from Frederick's chest. His blood covered her fingertips to the first joint, and Frederick moaned piteously.

"You are a singular man, Robert Archer," the night-slayer said. Her voice had quieted, her eyes suddenly looking almost human.

The door crashed open and Margery darted into the room. "What is happening? Frederick, what is the matter?"

"Get out," her husband gasped at her. "Robert has brought his tame night-slayer to kill us."

My night-slayer carefully sucked Frederick's blood from her forefinger. "I am not tame."

Margery did not appear to notice her. Her gaze fixed on the *drohner* that Frederick clutched in his shaking hands. "What is *that*?"

"The *drohner*," I said quietly. "I brought it back."

The color left Margery's face. She pressed one hand to her abdomen and the other to her mouth, then she turned and fled.

I went after her. For a small woman, Margery moved quickly. I did not catch up to her until she'd reached a bedchamber, where I found her vomiting into a basin.

"Margery," I asked in alarm. "What is wrong?" I touched her shaking back. "Is it the child?"

Margery did not answer. She lifted away from the basin, her face wet with tears and spittle. She reached for a towel and hid her face in it.

"Not the child," my night-slayer said behind me. "It is guilt."

"Margery stole the *drohner*," I said, finally understanding.

I remembered now that she'd paid me a visit a few days before I realized the thing had gone from the box I'd locked it into. I never liked her coming to my meager digs, and I'd rushed out to a tavern around the corner to bring her decent food and drink. She could easily have broken the flimsy lock of the box in my desk and taken the *drohner*.

In my gin-riddled state I'd not bothered looking at the thing or noticing that its hum in my heart had gone until I'd had the hankering to see it again. My devastation at finding the box empty had been horrible. I'd frantically searched my rooms, thinking I'd moved it and hadn't remembered. I'd ended up on the floor in wretched despair when I realized it was truly gone, and had drowned my sorrows in still more gin.

"That she did," the night-slayer said.

Margery lowered the towel. She looked pinched and old as she turned to the night-slayer. "How did you find it?"

The night-slayer spoke matter-of-factly. "I followed you when you last went to look at it. I suppose you couldn't resist making sure it was still safe. You hid it in the crypt of the Archer ancestors. Clever. You would have 'found' it when you laid your dear husband to rest."

Margery's eyes filled with fury as wild as any night-slayer's. "Frederick is brutal. I hate him."

The night-slayer did not change expression. "Your husband will weaken and die without the *drohner*. Everything he is comes from it."

"I *want* him to die," Margery spat. "I want the child to be Robert's. I want—I want *him*."

I stared at Margery in shock and anger. "You sent men after me to kill me. How can you say you want me and then do that?"

Margery shook her head, her wisps of curls trembling. "To frighten you. To stop you looking for the *drohner*. I never meant them to harm you. You have been good to me."

In the silence, two droplets of water fell from her wet fingers and spattered on the floor.

"Even if Freddy dies, I can never marry you," I said slowly. "The law forbids a man marrying his brother's wife. Doesn't matter if the brother is dead."

Margery's face was flushed with anger, her eyes wet. "My husband lives. With the return of the *drohner*, he will go on living. He will grow strong again. I can't bear it."

I pried the towel from Margery, set it aside, and took her hands. "Margery, I will not let him hurt you. Trust me —he will not lay a finger on you."

Margery's tears spilled from her eyes, her lips trembling in stark fear. "You cannot prevent him. You are not always here—Frederick does not listen to you. He doesn't respect you."

I was more resolute, and certain, as I looked into my sister-in-law's eyes than I had ever been. "I will protect you, Margery. I shall tell old Freddy that if he ever harms you, I will send for my night-slayer and let her play with him."

The night-slayer turned from where she'd been pacing a restless circuit of the room. "I am not tame, as I told you," she said in a hard voice. "Even if I do come when you bid me, I may be too hungry, too desperate to let you stop me killing him and draining him."

I gave her a dour look. "That is the risk Freddy will have to take. When he raises his hand against Margery, he will remember you reaching in for his heart tonight."

Margery's brown eyes were red-rimmed, her face blotchy with her weeping and illness. She looked beaten down and defeated, but I still saw the pretty young woman, all ringlets and soft smiles, who'd been introduced to me in a ballroom by Freddy, proud of his catch, all those years ago. I swore I would make her beautiful again.

I do not think Margery believed me when I said I could keep my brother in check, but I would make Freddy believe it.

My night-slayer was right: Frederick thought honor lay in a bit of stone, so easily taken, so easily lost. The night-slayer, a beast of violence and blood, had far more honor in her than Frederick ever would. For love of a child, an innocent, my night-slayer had curbed herself. For hope of a child, quiet Margery had committed two crimes in the eyes of the world.

I quit the room and strode back through the passage that led to Frederick's sitting room. The night-slayer followed. "I will not always come when you call," she warned me, sounding displeased.

"Frederick does not have to know that," I said with grim humor. "It is likely, if I put the fear of God in him, that you will not have to bother with him at all."

Candlelight sparkled on the night-slayer's sun-colored

hair. "Margery has bravery in her. She dealt her husband a mortal blow, stealing the *drohner*, and he could not do a thing about it. Margery did not like hurting you, I think, but she lived with that guilt to get to your brother. She will make him a formidable enemy."

I huffed a laugh. "Good. It is about time Margery had her own back. She will have him exactly where she wants him."

The night-slayer touched my hair. "And I have you." She released me and licked the last of Frederick's dried blood from her forefinger.

I gave her a startled look, but my night-slayer only smiled.

Androcles had never completely tamed his lion.

A MATTER AT NEW YEAR'S

A ROBERT ARCHER PARANORMAL MYSTERY NOVELLA

CHAPTER ONE

December 31, 1823

L ights whirled around me, or perhaps that was the brandy.

I reveled in a pool of laughter and warmth, light and false bravado that kept out the cold darkness of New Year's Eve.

In other words, I danced at a New Year's ball in the heart of Mayfair, held by a countess for the cowards of the *haut ton*, who refused to face the night alone.

These included me, of course. I'd been invited on the strength of my connection to my brother, Frederick Archer, gentleman of an ancient noble family, who'd gained in stature since I'd helped him recover his honor not long ago.

The heir he'd recently placed in his nursery—cutting me out of inheriting the Archer riches—had raised his standing as well. Freddy was here too, but I avoided him by taking to the floor as much as I could.

My partner in this energetic country dance was a young lady with golden hair and a pointed face. She was the daughter of one of Freddy's cronies, a man who'd deigned to allow a younger son without much means to lead his daughter out to the set.

They lady was pretty, but she was an unmarried miss, so there would be no dalliance. Also, I had no intention of calling at her home tomorrow with a posy and a proposal, so I was careful not to be overly attentive.

Truth to tell, I had no business dancing with her at all, but it was New Year's, and I suppose she was being generous.

Laughter sounded as we circled, the hundreds of candles the countess could waste her money on keeping the darkness at bay. The occasional drip of hot wax stung my face, but that was a small price to pay for this well of safety.

The windows that lined both ends of the room showed the gaping maw of night that waited for us outside—New Year's Eve was particularly cold, dark, and prone to danger. London tried to tame it with gaslights on the streets, but those could only do so much and rendered the shadows between them darker still.

Inside, lights glittered, merriment flowed, and the dance came to an end. I bowed to the young lady, who curtsied enchantingly in return.

I'd put my hand forward to ask her to dance once more, or else lead her to a chair, whichever she wished, when the clock struck midnight.

"Welcome the New Year!" our host boomed.

A glass of champagne found its way into my hand and

into those of the dispersing dancers. We raised them, crying the New Year's toast. The orchestra began another lively song, and gentlemen kissed the ladies.

My young lady was expropriated by another gent, and I lost my chance at a kiss. I laughed as though I did not care and gulped down my champagne, pretending it was all in good fun.

The golden-haired angel disappeared, and I was left to converse with my brother's colleagues, who were as thick-witted as he.

With no chance for more dancing, especially not the waltz that had begun, I could either nod my head at Freddy's idiotic friends or quit the place. I drained my glass, handed it to a discreet footman, and chose retreat.

I ought to have stayed.

Darkness crouched before me as I exited the house, and I was not comfortable with it. At the end of my walk from Grosvenor Square to my club in Gower Street would be my empty room and lonely bed. Not the most auspicious way to begin the new year.

With the warmth of the ballroom and the fizz of champagne wrapped around me, I dared the frigid cold, telling myself I could keep to the lighted streets. A carriage was out of the question—Freddy would be highly displeased if I absconded with his, and I didn't have the extra funds for a hackney.

All would have been well, I told myself forever after, if only the lamps hadn't been out on a stretch of Portland Street. I viewed the welling blackness on that route and on impulse ducked down Queen Anne Street East, which would take me into Bloomsbury, where my club for former regimental officers lay.

Queen Anne Street had no lights either, I realized belatedly. A glow shone at the end of it, and I made for that as fast as I could.

Not until I'd nearly reached the light did I see that what I'd glimpsed was not a gas lamp at the end of the narrow lane or the light from a warm house. The glow came from a lantern held aloft by a man, illuminating him and his two companions.

The three lingered in a tiny passageway that led off Queen Anne Street, doing I knew not what, and I did not want to know. They were not ruffians—their suits could have come from the finest Bond Street tailors. But the scent that overlaid the normal odors of cologne, smoke, and brandy, was unearthly and terrifying.

They were not night-slayers, thank the good Lord. I'd have been dead in an instant if so. Night-slayers were also quite rare—not that this would be any comfort to me if I'd encountered one—and they never congregated with others.

I knew what these men were, though, and I considered them even more frightening than night-slayers. Night-slayers killed to satisfy hunger. These men would hunt for the sport of it. Possibly they'd destroy their prey in the end, when that prey was begging for mercy or death, or possibly they'd leave me to die slowly and in great pain.

They were were-beasts. Animals—wolves usually— who could appear as civilized gentlemen while they hunted the night.

I'd stumbled upon a gathering of them.

Of course, they saw me. I was in deep shadow, while they held the lantern, but they didn't need the light. They'd scent a petrified, half-drunk army lieutenant a long way off his patch without any trouble at all.

I started to run.

I heard my own footfalls echoing on the pavement, the opening to the next street tantalizingly distant. I'd have to navigate through a few more lanes before I reached Tottenham Court Road, where I would find a hackney, expense be damned.

"Stop him."

The rumbling command came from behind me, the voice gravelly and strong. I sprinted on, but I was no match for the speed of weres.

In two steps, they surrounded me, three large men in pristine coats and cravats, material stretched across arms and shoulders that would look misshapen under clothes not as well-tailored.

"Please," I wheezed, my words slurring with the alcohol I'd consumed. Though I'd eschewed gin for a while now, I still found brandy and champagne agreeable, more fool I. "I never saw you."

One of them reached for me, a rangy man with a sharp face and feral eyes that would bring me nightmares. I brought up my fists and defended myself as he attacked, not about to roll into a ball and let them do what they willed.

I'd battled Frenchmen on the Peninsula and at Waterloo, soldiers who'd have cheerfully bayonetted me and left me for dead if I'd let them. But they'd been men, like me, who'd folded over when I elbowed them in the gut, bled when I struck them in the face.

Against this were, I might have been punching a wall. Another of them began to laugh, the note of a wolf's howl in his voice, glee at making the kill.

They didn't need knives or other weapons to subdue me. The one I fought brought up a hand that had turned to a beast's paw, splitting his gloves. Razor-like claws came for me, and I knew I'd be dead in a few slashes.

I braced myself for bright pain to blossom in my abdomen, or for hot blood to spray from my throat.

Instead, I saw the man abruptly recede, as though grappling hooks had fixed into his fashionable coat and jerked him away from me. The other two gaped in as much amazement, and their leader shouted.

There was fear in that shout. In the next instant, the rangy man crashed into the wall behind him, and I felt very strong fingers under my arm.

"Run," a woman's voice advised me.

I hesitated a step, shock stilling me, and she pushed me off.

"Run, idiotic man."

I recognized the truth in her statement. She was giving me a reprieve, and I needed to take it.

I sprinted away, heading through the warren of streets toward Tottenham Court Road. I heard the scuffle behind me but knew I'd be half-witted to turn around to see what occurred.

The wide boulevard of the refreshingly normal Tottenham Court Road embraced me. Light not only from street lamps but in house windows and on hackney coaches warmed me, and I slowed my pace, trying to catch my breath. The ordinariness of the road returned my confidence somewhat, and I walked the remainder of the short way to Gower Street and the refuge of my club.

The remnants of a New Year's celebration continued in the common room down the hall from the foyer, where I shed my coat. I joined the festivities to finish calming my nerves, sipped more brandy, and congratulated myself on my narrow escape.

I'd never seen weres in the flesh before. Heard of them, yes, listened to stories of braggadocios claiming they'd hunted them.

I now knew those stories were false. The men who'd told them would never have stood a moment before even one of the three I'd encountered.

It was said that weres couldn't be killed with ordinary weapons. There was rumor that silver could take them down, but no one had verified this idea. I suppose if the theory were true, someone would be alive to relate that it had worked. However, if the three I'd seen tonight lived in London, they'd find it highly impractical to stay if they couldn't touch silver.

Why had they been lurking on a dark street in Marylebone dressed in the first stare of fashion? As far as I knew, there's never been sightings in this part of the metropolis. Weres tended to hunt the back streets of the East End and South London, where darkness and easy escape to nearby fields helped conceal them.

The logical part of my brain worked on the question of their presence while the other part, the one that had managed my survival through many chaotic battles, continued to be chillingly aware that I'd nearly died tonight.

Once I'd had enough brandy to restore some false courage, I bade the company good night. Almay, my closest friend, slurred a *Happy New Year* at me, and I returned the wish before I sought the stairs to my chamber.

Once there, I reposed in the chair before my meager fire for a while, in case Almay decided to step up to gossip with me before I fell asleep. He didn't.

I was still in the chair a long while later, my candle having guttered out, when I came awake, aware I was no longer alone.

She sat on the other side of the fireplace from me, where Almay often did, dying light flickering on her fine-boned face.

"Happy New Year, Robert Archer," she said in her contralto voice.

I swallowed nervously. "And to you." I had never learned her name, and I did not ask it now.

"Tell me." Her gaze was calm, as though she wasn't the deadliest person in this entire house full of hardened, well-trained soldiers. "What have you done to make a trio of were-beasts so interested in you?"

CHAPTER THREE

Nothing," was my instinctive reply. I ran through my head any possible ways the encounter had been my fault and came up with none. "I was walking home from a gathering and took a wrong turn."

"Hmm." She pinned me with her night-dark gaze, making it clear she didn't believe me. "You are prone to trouble, Lieutenant Archer."

"So everyone in my life has explained to me." Silence fell between us for a moment, then I drew a breath and told her what I truly thought she'd come here to learn. "She is growing rapidly, almost a young lady."

The child in question was about five years old if I calculated correctly, but I mothers like to hear soppy things about their children.

Her eyes softened the slightest bit. "I know. I see her—from afar, of course. I thought you had ceased visiting that house."

I had, once Lizzie, who looked after the night-slayer's little girl, had told me to go.

"I return once a year. I'm responsible for the mite and make the excuse of dropping around funds to keep her." Lizzie also had borne a child who looked like me, though none, including Lizzie's husband or the lad himself, had ever remarked upon it.

The night-slayer's brows rose. "Good of you."

"I keep my promises." I longed for more brandy but decided it prudent not to indulge. One needs one's instincts sharp to deal with a night-slayer.

The trouble was, my lady night-slayer looked like anyone's maiden sister. Her golden curls were dressed in a simple fashion, drawn up in back, with curls framing her face. Her gown was dark blue velvet, covered by a brown coat that looked woolen and warm. A matching brown bonnet lay in her lap.

A man conversing with her might let his guard down. I made certain never to.

"I've observed that you have honor," she said. "Make certain you never lose it."

Correction, she was like anyone's maiden sister, ready to scold.

"You look well," I said, to change the subject. "Are you?"

Surprised that I'd ask flickered across her face. "I've learned how to keep myself. Why should you be concerned?"

I managed a shrug. "Fellow feeling?"

"I am a night-slayer."

"And a mother," I reminded her. "You make certain your daughter is cared for and you stop in the middle of the night to keep me from being killed by were-beasts. Forgive me if that makes me polite."

She was on her feet, hanging over my chair in an instant. I'd never seen her move. The maiden sister was gone, and now her shell barely concealed the monster within.

"You confound me, Archer. Go to sleep."

I fought the command. Nodding off while a night-slayer, a creature who fed on warm blood, hovered inches from one's face was not a good idea.

The next thing I knew, I was lying on my bed, fully dressed, though minus my boots, a blanket spread over me. Feeble daylight peeked through the window, telling me New Year's Day had dawned.

I was alone, the night-slayer nowhere in sight.

I pried myself out of bed, shed the wrinkled suit that my friend Derek Chase had insisted I purchase from his tailor, and pulled on my own more sensible clothes. I rinsed my face in the basin, the water cold as a winter night, and managed to tie a cravat and brush my dark hair into something tame.

As I dressed, I searched my neck and other parts of my body for telltale bites, but found none, to my relief. The night-slayer had once more or less vowed not to feed on me, but she might have needed a quick repast.

Bloodshot brown eyes stared back at me from the mirror as I settled the cravat and re-buttoned my waist-coat, which I'd done up wrongly the first time. I'd given up strong drink for the most part, but celebrations with other revelers always weakened my resolve.

When I reached the breakfast room downstairs, I saw

by its tall case clock that it was eleven thirty in the morning. The early risers, whom the rest of us found baffling, had come and gone, and my fellow mid-morning diners were dragging themselves through a light meal.

These, to my surprise included Daniel Almay, fellow lieutenant of my regiment, who was usually one of the early risers. He looked far too fresh to have enjoyed a raucous New Year's Eve—his black hair was neat and shining, his blue eyes clear and bright.

"Archer," he greeted me. "Best of the New Year to you."

I only grunted a reply. I ignored the indifferent food at the sideboard and plopped into a chair at Almay's otherwise empty table. One of the attendants who worked here for low wages slammed a cup down by my elbow and a tarnished silver pot next to that before retreating.

I poured thick coffee into the cup, trying not to obviously inhale the heady aroma.

"*Is* it morning?" I asked Almay when I could speak. "I hadn't noticed."

"Very amusing. The trouble with giving up strong drink is that when one has it again, one is unable to stand it. Now, I drank whiskey all the night long and am none the worse for wear."

"Thank you, my friend." I gulped coffee, which was lukewarm, but at this point I did not care. "Please, speak louder. My splitting head demands it."

Almay's laugh clanged through my senses and increased my anguish. "I am pleased you arrived safely home in spite of yourself."

I saluted him with my cup and continued drinking. My face had escaped a battering somehow, but my arms and torso had been quite bruised, I'd discovered while inspecting my flesh for teeth marks this morning. I shuddered to contemplate what would have become of me if my lady hadn't intervened.

Almay leaned toward me, though his voice was as booming as ever. "I have a strange tale to relate. A mate told me of it this morning."

"This morning?" I asked with little interest. "We have just established it is morning at all. You do not mean earlier than this?"

"Yes, indeed. I went out for a brisk stroll a few hours ago."

"Dear Lord, how I loathe you." I drained my cup and trickled more coffee into it. My body was slowly coming awake, which meant it revealed to me how sore I was.

"Long walks and cold baths, my friend," Almay said with his characteristic gusto. "Keeps a man sound. But it is an old argument with you. Anyway, my mate is a junior barrister in Middle Temple. His leader is a celebrated silk, he makes certain to drop several times into any conversation. Their clerk always sniffs the wind for potential criminal cases. He heard of one today."

"The lot of you were out infernally early," I said in impatience. "It is why I chose not to go into law."

"Yes, the army is so much better for a restful night's sleep. Can I tell you what my mate said? It is more exciting than watching you drown yourself in coffee."

I relented. "Your pardon. I overindulged when, as you say, I was not used to it, and my mood is foul. Continue."

Almay bent even closer, his cravat almost touching his empty plate. "Perkins—that's my friend—said his clerk has come across nothing less than a gruesome murder. Of a respectable gent, in Howland Street, near the Tottenham Court Road, shortly after midnight. They're saying the poor fellow was killed by were-beasts. What do you think of that?" He frowned in sudden consternation. "Archer? You all right? You've gone bloodless."

I couldn't move. Almay had faded, and I again saw the three weres in their costly clothes, again felt the paralyzing terror that had snapped me sober for a moment. Saw the eyes of my attacker, yellow-gray and narrowing to predatory slits, his hand sprouting razor-like claws.

"I saw them," I choked out.

Almay gaped at me. "Saw who? You don't mean the were-beasts? You witnessed the murder?"

"No, no." Thank God for that. "But yes, the were-beasts. They were lurking in the dark near Queen Anne Street. They must have killed that chap right after I got away from them."

Almay eased back in his chair, his cravat having escaped the dregs of his morning meat pie. "Are you certain you saw weres? You must have been in a deep state of inebriation by then."

I shook my head, an action I regretted. "I drank even more when I reached here, happy to have escaped with my life. I did see them, three of the wretches. Dressed like they were flitting through clubs in St. James's."

"We're a long way from St. James's," Almay said. "How did you get away, if there were three? You can run like the wind, I know, but they're hunters."

I couldn't explain without bringing in my night-slayer,

which I had told no one about, not even my closest friends.

"Sheer luck," I said truthfully. "They must not have been interested in me. Perhaps they were lying in wait for this other fellow and didn't have time to dismember me properly."

"Very well, I believe you." Almay slipped a flask from his pocket and dolloped whatever was in it into my coffee. "You look spooked enough to be telling the truth. How do you know it was *before* they went after the other man, and not after?"

"Because their suits were clean." I sipped the coffee, now laced with whiskey, rendering it more drinkable. "If they'd killed a fellow, they'd have had blood all over their clothing. And be sated enough to not bother with me."

Almay made a face. "Gruesome. But perhaps you could be of help. I predict there will be a manhunt for these weres—or a beast hunt, I suppose. You could describe them to the Runners, give them a start."

The whiskey-dosed coffee made me feel marginally better. "Or I could describe them to you, you could describe them to the Runners, and I could go back to bed and never leave this house again."

Almay chuckled. "True, but you have an honest face and a family name. They're more likely to believe you than me."

As I pondered his suggestion, I again wondered how close I'd come to death last night. The weres had let me go without pursuit, I assumed because of my lady night-slayer's intervention. But perhaps I was right that they'd been more interested in this other unfortunate chap. I'd possibly been a distraction at best.

"Tell you what," I said. "I'll speak to your friend—Perkins, is it? Your junior barrister. If he thinks my tale coherent enough to interest a magistrate, he may take it to them."

Almay considered this and nodded. "I will fix an appointment." He peered at me critically. "You ought to eat something, Archer. You look peaky."

I finished off my second dose of coffee, scooping up the dregs of whiskey with my tongue. "This will do for me. Anything else will come only back up."

"A walk, then," he persisted. "It's crisp outside. Will be just the thing."

"Yes, shriveling my balls in the cold wind will make me feel better." I was suddenly restless, though, not wanting to sit still. I rose. "But I think I will. Join me?"

Almay sat back with his own coffee, taking a comfortable sip. "I've already been virtuously up and about, I've told you. I'll finish here and have a nap."

"You are a bastard," I said clearly. Others glanced up, noted it was me speaking to the grinning Almay, and ignored us.

"As always." Almay saluted me with his cup. "To your good health."

I said something unkind about *his* health and took myself away.

The doorman fetched my coat and hat, and I stepped out into a breeze that Almay had called crisp and I called a blustering gale. The narrow street was in deep shade—we might see a sliver of sunshine about noon, if any appeared through the clouds at all.

I moved at a rapid clip along Gower Street and north towards Regent's Park. I made my way around the crescent at its entrance and into the vast green space that held a botanical garden and other amusements.

Others were out enjoying the relatively dry day, a welcome respite from winter rain, even if the wind was bloody cold.

My head continued to pound, but my roiling stomach calmed as I wandered the park in air only partly tainted by chimney smoke. I'd have to travel to Hampstead Heath to find an even clearer patch, but I didn't have the stamina to journey that far today. At least the wind pushed the worst of the muck out of the city.

I came off a path near the canal, turned a corner among a stand of trees, and nearly ran into a large gentleman in a well-tailored greatcoat. His cravat was blindingly white, his hat one I could never afford.

He was huge and strong, with narrowing gray eyes and a scent I'd never forget. I'd first noted it last night, in the choked lane on my way home from the New Year's Eve gathering.

"Bloody hell," I burst out.

I turned to sprint away but was hemmed in by his two friends, both slightly less large than their leader but no less dangerous.

"I'll make barely a morsel, I assure you," I said as I debated how to escape. "I've had too much drink and not enough sustenance."

I could charge into the copse next to us, I thought in

desperation. If I zigzagged through the trees, I might be able to gain a more open and populous area, discouraging pursuit. Either that or dive into the canal and hope that werewolves couldn't swim.

"Mr. Archer." The leader put his hand—not a paw, thank heavens—on my shoulder. "We wish to speak to you. There is a matter in which you can help us."

His voice was a deep rumble, nearly shaking the ground beneath my feet.

"Help?" I demanded. "Is that what you told the other fellow, before you tore him to pieces?"

To my surprise, the leader's expression became distressed. "This is the matter, exactly, Mr. Archer. We didn't kill him. We need your help to prove that we did not."

CHAPTER THREE

I stared at him, dumbfounded. I wasn't certain whether I was more surprised that beasts who ran down their prey were worried they'd be accused of murder, or at the leader's insistence that I could save them.

"Why on earth do you think *I* can help?" I asked when I at last found my voice.

"You've tamed a night-slayer," the were who'd attacked me first last night said. He was more rangy than the leader, with a lean face and pale wiry hair drawn into an old-fashioned tail.

"She isn't tame," I informed him and only got a curled lip in response.

"She fought for you," the leader said. "That either means she's taken you for her pet, in which case she'd feed from you. Or, you have ensorcelled her. You do not have the look of a one who is a night-slayer's slave. Such men are willing to crawl at their master's or mistress's feet and begin to lose interest in the rest of life. You have too much color in your face for her to be feeding on you."

"She is not," I could say truthfully. "But nor have I ensorcelled her, not that I'd know how to even if I wanted to. I did her a good turn once, is all. She is grateful."

The third man, who hadn't spoken, snorted laughter at this. The leader silenced him with a stern look.

"Regardless, you move about the supernatural world unharmed," the leader continued. "A formidable feat. I vow to you on my ancestors' bones that we did not kill that man. But all will assume we did."

I was starting to believe him, and not because of his vow or the sincerity in his voice. Predators could be enticing.

I believed him because, as I'd told Almay, when I'd encountered them, it was evident they hadn't just walked away from a slaughter. What they'd been plotting in that alley, I didn't know, but they'd been blood-free and appeared as though they'd recently strolled out of a club.

Also, the fact that the body had been discovered at all —lying in the street and not dredged, half-consumed, from the river many days hence—pointed to their probable innocence. Such corpses shredded by were-beasts had been pulled out of the Thames before.

"I am not yet convinced I can help you," I said to them. "Whether I believe you or not."

A flicker of relief shone in the leader's eyes, as though he'd expected me to be more stubborn than I was. "*I am* convinced of it. Shall we speak in someplace warmer? A tavern, perhaps?"

He was right that it was brutally cold, and now that my headache was dying off, I was growing hungry. A tavern would allow me to slake my thirst as well, and I'd feel safer in a crowd instead of alone with three weres on a canal towpath.

"Very well," I conceded. "I believe there is a decent tavern around the corner from park's edge, not far from here."

The leader huffed a laugh. "No. We will go somewhere we'll be welcome. Come."

He swung around and started down the path at a good clip. The two surging behind me gave me no choice but to follow him.

The weres took me out of the park at its southern edge and to the road from Paddington, a busy thoroughfare this time of day. I thought we'd continue to stride through the streets, but the lead were halted before a large carriage that waited in a lane off the well-trafficked road.

I'd never have thought horses would be easy around weres, but this team of finely matched grays stood calmly under the watchful eye of a coachman. The coachman, a squat but nimble specimen, jerked upright from where he leaned on railings flanking a house and yanked open the carriage's door.

He glared hard at me with yellow-pupiled eyes, and I realized he was another were. Of what sort, I could not decide.

The leader gave the coachman some direction I did not hear, because I was being bundled inside by the other two while he spoke.

Soon enough we were all squashed into a warm and sumptuous coach, me stuck between the two seconds while the leader reposed across from us. The carriage jerked into the street as soon as the doors shut, taking me who knew where.

We journeyed eastward for a long while, until I thought the coach was going all the way to Islington, before it turned south and headed back into the heart of the metropolis.

Our eastward journey presently resumed, taking us past Smithfield and Finsbury Square, skirting the City itself. No question about where we were going was answered, and eventually, I ceased bothering.

The streets grew less salubrious as we traveled, and when we finally halted, I saw that we were well into Whitechapel. The weres descended in a lane I'd be hesitant to walk through alone—I detected men lurking in the shadows ready to part anyone foolish enough to venture here with his purse, his watch, his clothes, and possibly his life.

The weres moved confidently, but then, they could. Who would challenge them?

Despite my misgivings, we did indeed enter a tavern, a surprisingly cozy one for this part of London. A fire danced on a hearth, benches lined an inglenook near it, and tavern tables of polished wood filled the floor. A landlord, who was human, immediately signaled the plump young woman who moved about the room to fetch tankards and carry them to the table the leader chose.

"They do a fine beefsteak here," the leader informed me as we sat. "Bring my friend a plate." The waitress, as though finding nothing unusual, nodded and departed.

The rangy were slid his chair out beyond the rest of ours, as though he were guarding the pack. The third man, who had dark red hair and a thin beard, also kept a watchful eye on our surroundings.

The weres waited in silence until the barmaid returned bearing food. She set a plate of roast meat swimming in dark juices in front of me, along with a few potatoes and a hunk of bread for sopping up the liquids. The walk and my subsequent fright had now driven away the hangover, and I tucked in.

The lead were-beast was right: the beefsteak was excellent, even if I suspected it had been roasted last night and kept warm in the kitchen for today's meals.

The leader also accepted a plate from the barmaid, though the others waved her off. The leader removed a removed a silk pouch from a pocket inside his coat, extracting from it a silver knife and fork.

"You look surprised, Archer," he said as he cut into the beef. "Did you think we devoured our meals raw? Possibly with the animal still warm?"

"Something like that." I shut out the picture he painted so I could enjoy my meal. The fact that his cutlery was silver also put paid to the idea that the metal harmed them. "Does the landlord here know who you are?"

"That we are were-beasts?" the leader answered easily. "Yes. A friend of mine owns the place. He's a were-cat himself."

The rangy man snarled softly, like a dog would when he spied a feline in his territory.

"You must have powerful friends," I observed as I dragged bread through the gravy and stuffed it into my mouth. "Surely one of them could help you better than I can."

"Your friend Lieutenant Almay is acquainted with a barrister," the leader said instead of answering me. "We might have need of his services. If you prove trustworthy, I will ask that you offer him our fee."

My eyes widened. "A barrister to defend a were? He's junior to a silk, and both of them will be more likely to oppose you. Anyway, how do you know about Almay and his acquaintances?"

"We found out about you." The man's voice held a warning note, reminding me how dangerous he was, despite this warm tavern and tasty repast. "After our encounter with you last night, we made it our business to discover who you were. Who your family is, who are your friends …"

I was glad I'd downed most of the food by now, because I promptly lost my appetite. "If you think to threaten me—"

"Calm yourself, my friend. I am only telling you in order to save explanations later. When I saw you had a night-slayer in your pocket, I knew I needed to learn all I could about you. I like to know what I'm up against when we walk the night."

"I am mostly asleep when you walk the night." I slurped the ale, which was also surprisingly good.

The leader regarded me as though I'd just confirmed his suspicions that I was an idiot. "Even so."

"I am at a disadvantage here," I said. "You know my name and where I live, but I have no idea what you call yourselves."

The leader shrugged. "Fair enough. My name is Kieran Hacault. The ginger-haired gent there is Ross McCall.

And my personal bodyguard, Seamus Brodie." He indicated the lanky man with yellow eyes who'd done his best to gut me last night.

They nodded to me in turn, and they weren't friendly nods. I wondered why a were-beast, a formidable killer, needed a bodyguard, but I decided not to ask.

"Why else should I believe you didn't kill that man?" I asked. "Can you prove it?"

"No, which is why you need to intercede for us," Kieran said.

"If we'd done it, there'd be nothing left," the man called Ross said. "And we'd have disposed of the corpse. But we'd no reason to kill a random gent wandering that part of London."

"You tried to kill *me*." I took another sip of ale, aware I sat uncomfortably close to them.

Kieran shook his head. "No, we tried to stop you rushing away shouting that weres were on the streets. We didn't need attention called to us. Seamus would have clouted you and left you unconscious, nothing more."

Seamus sent me an evil glance, and I felt no better.

"I am grateful my own bodyguard was there to look out for me. Not that she comes when called," I added hastily.

I'd noticed, as Kieran's carriage had brought me across London, a young woman in a brown cloak and bonnet, her head always down, strolling among the throngs. She'd disappear for a time, then the coach would turn a corner, and I'd see her again, sometimes ahead of us. How she accomplished this feat, I did not know, but I was grateful she stayed near.

"You have the luck of the devil," Kieran said. "Do not squander it. What I require of you, Mr. Archer, is to convince this barrister friend of your Lieutenant Almay that he'd have a better case if he defends us. That he can gather evidence that proves we had nothing to do with the death. Of course, this is assuming we will even be brought to trial."

Families of a victim could bring a prosecution suit against those they believed had killed their loved one, even if the Runners didn't make an arrest. I hadn't seen any Runners or foot patrollers as we'd made our way through London, despite Almay's claim there'd soon be a hunt for the weres responsible. They certainly hadn't been following Kieran through Regent's Park.

"You might escape the courts altogether," I said. "Human watchmen, and even the Runners, don't like to tangle with weres."

"They've learned to leave us be," Kieran acknowledged. "But they might choose to rampage through all our communities, to show the people of London they are doing something about the crime. I would like our names cleared, regardless. It is important."

Kieran's eyes became those of a predator as he spoke. He did not lie when he said it was of great import, but I equally knew he would not tell me why.

What I did know was that Kieran had treated me to a very good meal at an out-of-the-way tavern in Whitechapel, where the proprietor and his assistants understood that Kieran and his colleagues were werebeasts. Or at least knew how to serve them without panic. I had no doubt that if any of the non-weres in this tavern threatened Kieran and his mates in any way, they'd not live long.

It was also evident that Kieran knew my every move and could run me to ground any time he liked, night-slayer or no.

I scraped up the last of my meal, took another long swallow of ale, and heaved a sigh as I set down the tankard.

"Well," I said. "I will see what I can do."

———

KIERAN PUT ME IN A HACKNEY AFTER MY UNLOOKED-FOR luncheon, but to my relief, he did not suggest that he or the others accompany me home.

While the horses pulling Kieran's own coach had stood calmly as the weres boarded it, the hackney's steed shied nervously when Kieran drew near. The driver scowled down at him, ready to tell him to bugger off, but Kieran tipped his hat, bade me good day, and returned to the tavern.

I was left to digest my meal and decide how the devil I would prove that three were-beasts, reputedly killing machines, had not murdered the chap in the lane.

Kieran and his companions had likely killed before—I was certain Seamus had. If they were executed for this murder, even if they hadn't committed it, would not justice have been done for any others they'd harmed?

I suppressed a shiver, knowing I couldn't simply hand them over to the law.

First, the execution for weres was grisly. Burning a

person alive hadn't occurred since the sixteenth century, when heretics had been put on pyres, but exceptions were made for weres. It was thought that they couldn't truly die until their entire bodies were consumed by flame, nothing left but ash. If they suffered on the way, well, that made up for the anguish of the people they'd torn apart.

Second, if Kieran and his mates *weren't* responsible, then someone out there was. The lane where the man had died was too close to the ones I trudged daily. If a killer lurked in my part of London, I wanted him flushed out.

"I'm not a Runner," I muttered. "I don't know how I can find a murderer if they can't."

The hackney hit a hole in the road, jolting the carriage hard. I felt a brief and icy draft and glanced up to see if a window had bounced open, but they were all tightly fastened.

I looked again at the seat opposite me, to find her reposing on it.

I suppressed a yelp. "God's teeth, woman. One day you will make my heart stop."

The night-slayer peered at me from under her bonnet, her eyes going darker still. "On that day, I will feast."

I could never decide whether she teased me or was serious.

"You've been following me," I stated.

"Of course I have. You leapt into a carriage with three wolves, and I could not be certain you'd come out again. Why do you ever behave like a fool?"

"They gave me no choice."

She frowned at me, clearly disappointed in my powers

of thought. "You could have run, shouted, fought, screamed for the watch. Screamed for me."

"I knew none of those things would save my life, if they chose to end it," I answered with a calmness I did not feel. "I had no idea you were anywhere near, and I can't shout your name if I do not know it."

She ignored this last statement. "They want you to prove they didn't kill the man."

She'd have found this out somehow, so I didn't stare in amazement at her perception. "Yes, but I don't know how the devil I am to do it."

"Have you seen the body?"

"No." I'd been pondering a way to have a look at it, or at least obtain a good description. "I'll be speaking to Almay's barrister friend. He might have more details about how the man died. Then I suppose I could haunt the streets and discover who saw what last night. But the Runners must have already done such a thing."

"The Runners believe that weres did it and have not bothered with much investigation," she said in disgust. "Once they decide which were-beasts were responsible, they'll have Hacault and his seconds rounded up. If they don't simply arrest all the weres they can find and sort it out later."

So Kieran had speculated. "Do weres stand trial like the rest of us?" I asked. "In the dock at the Old Bailey, while wigged judges solemnly pronounce sentence?"

My lady shook her head. "Supernatural beings—if they can be caught—are taken to Southwark to a place worse than Newgate will ever be. They are tried in a room that has been guarded by magical wards to prevent their escape. The verdict is almost always guilty, and they are taken to their place of execution soon afterward."

I heard the bleakness in her voice as she explained. "Were you ever imprisoned there?"

"No. I am careful. But I've known those who have been." Her face hardened, forestalling any more questions. "I have no fondness for weres, who consider themselves superior beings, but I'd not wish that fate on anyone."

"I believed Kieran when he told me they were innocent." I shrugged. "If I'd met the other two without him, I might not."

"Kieran Hacault is a compelling man, but don't be too beguiled. He spared you because of me, and because he is interested in you."

"Wondering why I have a night-slayer leaping to my defense?" I glanced out of the grime-streaked window at streets that fog crept over. The wind had died, allowing moisture from the river to overtake us. "I wonder that myself, most days."

I felt the chill breeze again, and when I looked back at the seat, she was gone.

I pulled dusty curtains over the window, leaned against the lumpy cushions, and closed my eyes. "And I wonder how the devil she does *that*."

The cold hackney couldn't answer me, and I rode the rest of the way in silence, my thoughts tangled.

———

When I returned to the club, I ran down Almay and told him I'd like to speak with his barrister friend today if possible. Almay was agog to know why I was suddenly in a hurry, but he knew it would do him no good to quiz me about it.

He went out in his energetic way while I returned to my chamber to catch up on sleep. This time no night-slayers appeared by my fireplace and no weres turned up to bother me either.

By the time I dressed for the evening, brushed my hair into some semblance of order, and went downstairs, Almay presented me with a slim, dark-haired young man who shook my hand with enthusiasm.

"Interested in my sordid murder, are you?" he asked.

"This is Perkins," Almay said to me. "He has no manners."

"Jonathan Perkins, junior barrister of the Middle Temple," the young man informed me. "In the chambers of Sir Nathan Linton."

He said this last as though I ought to be impressed, but as I had no idea who Linton was, I merely nodded.

"Thank you for agreeing to speak to me," I said.

"Almay said you were an old army chum. What do you wish to know?"

I led Perkins and Almay into what passed for the library—a room with a shelf full of books—which most of the gentlemen here avoided. The inhabitants of this club were more interested in food and conversation, leaving the books to the few who bothered with them.

The chamber was empty, and I gestured Perkins to the worn armchairs in the middle of it. Almay fetched brandy from a decanter on a nearby table, and we sipped companionably.

When I asked Perkins to tell me all, he began. "What I know about this murder is that a chap called James Copeland was found with his throat slit a few streets from here. Almay says you were walking that way around the same moment. You didn't do it, did you?" His eyes twinkled.

I shook my head. "Last night, I wasn't in a fit state to hold onto a knife, let alone try to strike someone else with it. Also, at the time, I was being assailed by were-beasts, escaping from them by the skin of my teeth."

Perkins' mouth formed an O. "You *saw* them? Truly?"

"I not only saw them, I fought myself free of them." I took a sip of brandy, happy that both my stomach and my head had regained their peace. "Today, they spoke to me again and asked me if you'd be willing to defend them in court."

CHAPTER FOUR

I had the satisfaction of rendering both Almay and Perkins speechless for several moments.

"Defend them?" Perkins squeaked.

"The Runners might believe they committed the crime," I said after another calm sip of brandy. "I believe they did not."

Almay regarded me as though he'd always suspected I was mad, and I'd at last proved it. "This morning you were happy you escaped them with your life. Are you saying you sought them out to ask whether they killed the fellow?"

"No, no." I waved a languid hand. "They took me out for beefsteak—quite a good one, I must say—and related their side of the tale. They never saw Copeland and didn't kill him. The crime seems all wrong for them anyway."

Perkins listened, wide-eyed. "They murdered him because they are hot-blooded killers. I knew Copeland slightly, which makes it all the more dismaying."

"They might be hot-blooded killers," I conceded. "But

that doesn't mean they slaughter everyone in London who turns up dead. There are plenty of footpads and ruffians to do that."

"I suppose." Perkins watched me with interest. "What else did they say?"

"Only that they know they'll be accused of the crime, regardless. They are allowed some defense, and they'd like a good barrister to help them."

"Hmm."

The fact that Perkins didn't dismiss my request as ravings, or hysterically declare there was no way a were-beast could be innocent, raised him in my estimation. He was actually thinking the problem through before reacting.

"Are you certain they didn't bewitch you?" Almay asked me. "Seduce you with excellent beefsteak?"

"And ale," I said. "I could take you to the tavern," I offered to Perkins. "They frequent the place. No one there was very alarmed by them."

Almay snorted a laugh and took a gulp of brandy. "Likely because they have taken it over as their territory. I imagine none dare oppose them."

I had to admit the possibility. While no one at the tavern had behaved as though they'd been terrified of Kieran and his friends, none had been overtly friendly either.

"I'd have to be absolutely certain of their guiltlessness," Perkins said. "One must guard one's reputation. If it's put about that I defend weres who actually do butcher human beings, I'll never wear silk. Might be shunned altogether.

So, they have to be not only innocent of *this* crime, but blameless in all others."

"They seem to prefer roast beef above all else," I said, though I truly had no idea whether they indulged themselves on human flesh or not. I'd believe it of Seamus, anyway.

Perkins's eyes shone. "If I could make a judge declare that they are pure as the driven snow, think what that would do for me. I could be the next Cicero."

"Or, you'd have every were-beast in London commanding you to make *them* look pure as well," Almay pointed out. "I think you are both mad."

"I'll not call you as a witness then." Perkins grinned. "Let me ponder some more, and then I'll have you introduce me, if I decide it's wise. The best thing would be to find the person who did murder Copeland, so I could pull that out of my sleeve in front of a judge."

Perkins gazed at me hopefully, as though I knew the killer's identity and where he could be found.

"I have no evidence for that," I said with regret. "Only reasonable doubt the weres didn't do it."

"If you give me the true killer, I'll make certain your new mates don't go down for it," Perkins promised.

"Me?" I blinked at him. "How am I to do that?"

Perkins shrugged. "Runners usually bully everyone in sight until someone confesses. I suppose you could question whoever happened to be in the area and also the victim's friends and family, in case one of them followed the chap and cut him down, blaming it on a footpad. Or in this instance, weres."

"You certainly could do that, Archer," Almay agreed.

"You're good at poking your nose into people's lives. Remember how you searched high and low for your family's *drohner*? Found it, too, didn't you?"

The *drohner* was a magical stone that held a family's power and strength, a foolish bit of sorcery, but so traditional an ancient family like mine would never think to discard it. Ours had once gone missing, and I'd spent a few years hunting for it. I had finally located it, but only with help I couldn't discuss.

"You are asking rather a lot," I said, pained.

"As are you." Perkins sat back, a grin on his face. "Defending were-beasts. Either I'll be hailed as a genius or my name will be blackened forever."

"Well then." I raised my glass to him. "We'd better get on with finding a murderer."

———

INSTEAD OF RUSHING OUT IMMEDIATELY TO DISCOVER MORE about Mr. Copeland, I restored my greatcoat and took a walk down Gower Street and through Bedford Square, making my way south. I avoided the dangerous areas of St. Giles and Seven Dials and arrived at the livelier thoroughfare of St. Martin's Lane.

I knocked on the door of a small house off that lane, accosted by light, noise, and the odors of cooking when the door was yanked open.

A lad of about ten years stared up at me. "What yer want?" he demanded before he recognized me. "Uncle Robbie? It's Uncle Robbie!" He declared this at the top of his voice as he dragged me unceremoniously into the house.

The front room held an assortment of children of various ages plus a large man who heaved himself from a battered sofa. "Now then, Robbie."

"Ooh, look what the rats dragged in." Lizzie Greene, wife of the good-natured giant, gave me a hard look from the doorway to the next room, from where the smells of roasting and baking emitted.

"You mean the cat, mum," the boy who'd answered the door declared.

"I know what I said, love."

Lizzie had sent me away about a year ago, ending the cozy arrangement we'd had, but I hadn't minded all that much. It had been time for both of us to move on.

"I bring New Year's gifts." I pulled a small bag from my coat and brandished it.

The boy darted up the stairs that rose from the corner of the room. "Oi! You lot, get down here! Uncle Robbie's brought presents."

"It isn't much," I said apologetically.

"Not much is a lot to them," Jack rumbled. "Kind of ye, Robbie."

I shrugged, pretending that their warm home didn't render my cold rooms even emptier and colder. The family had only what Jack managed to earn as a man-of-all-work and Lizzie did taking in washing and piecework sewing, but they made up for it with a closeness my family had always lacked. My affair with Lizzie had been a refuge for a while, she always having room in her heart for one more.

The seven children gathered around, eager and smiling, not without some pushing, shoving, and grappling. I handed out my treasures—sixpences, one for each. The lads and lasses seized them as though they were gold.

"You'll spoil them," Lizzie admonished as her brood cheered me.

I shrugged. I hadn't given the lad who had my shape of face any more than the others, because none knew but Lizzie and me. She'd told me to keep it that way, and I always obliged, as much as my heart burned. When he was grown … well, we'd think on that later.

I did have a special gift for the small girl they called Anne, who all acknowledged was adopted. She had a mop of golden curls and a pair of clear blue eyes, telling me what color her mother's eyes had been before they'd changed.

For her, I'd found a dolly made of papier mâché and dressed in an exquisite gown that the toy seller assured me was the height of fashion. When I laid the doll in Anne's arms, she gasped and held it close.

As Anne was everyone's pet, the other lasses, who were older than her, didn't look on in envy. They assured her they'd find a place for the dolly to sleep and help keep her clean and nice.

"You're too kind for your own good, Robbie," Lizzie said as the children leapt up the stairs, proclaiming to each other as loudly as possible what they'd do with their sixpence. "Especially to her."

"Anne ain't yours," Jack added. He'd resumed his seat, the most comfortable in the house, but the poor sod worked like a dog and deserved the rest. "She don't resemble you in the slightest."

"He means, why'd ye take so much trouble about her?" Lizzie interpreted.

I shrugged. "I found the poor mite. I feel responsible for her."

"She's a lucky lass, then," Lizzie said.

My heart warmed, as much as I told it not to. Lizzie had loved me once, I'd been certain, but then, she loved everyone. I doubt I'd been singled out as special.

"You'll have to do something about her when she's grown," Jack informed me. "She'll want to be married or learn a trade or such. I don't think she was born in the gutter, even if you found her there."

Anne had become as rough and tumble as their own children, but I supposed Jack and Lizzie, who knew the ways of the streets, were right. Which re-fired my curiosity both about her mother and who the girl's true father might have been.

"I'll look after her," I promised. I had only a vague idea what that would entail, but the lass was only five years old. Plenty of time to think it through, or so I told myself.

I hadn't brought gifts for Lizzie and Jack, because I knew they wouldn't take them, and also, I didn't want to behave as though I was Lizzie's protector.

Jack was a good-natured man and had never said a word, but looking into his eyes as he rose to send me off, I saw that he knew. That he'd always known and had indulged Lizzie in enjoying herself while he slept off his hard day.

He and Lizzie shared a bond I'd never found with anyone, and Lizzie hadn't shared that bond with me.

"Keep yourselves well in the coming year," I said to them both. "My best wishes to you."

"You as well, Robbie," Lizzie said kindly. She was always kind to me.

Jack didn't shake my hand, but he nodded. "Look after yourself, now."

"I will. Good night." I made myself leave the warm retreat and return to the unwelcome streets before the hour grew too late.

The walk home was colder and darker than the stroll down had been. Not only had the evening become more chill, but the contrast between Lizzie's contented life and my existence was stark.

They'd confirmed tonight that they expected me to take charge of Anne at some point in her life. That meant I needed to stay alive to do so—I couldn't fall prey to weres or to whoever was trying to shove the blame for a murder onto them. I would have to find the answer to this mystery quickly.

I also wondered very much about my lady night-slayer's history. She'd never given me any clue about what her life had been before I'd stumbled upon her, but I suspected she came from a gently born family, who'd given her up for dead once she'd been turned.

Would such people care for her child? Or were any of them still alive at all?

With my thoughts equal parts curious to equal parts gloomy, I reached the club unscathed. I was very certain, however, that I'd glimpsed Seamus in the shadows, tracking my every move. Protecting me? Or deciding I ought to be killed after all?

I tried to erase my unease with brandy in the card room, but I wasn't in the mood for games and sought my bed early.

In the small hours of the morning, as freezing draft woke me from a half-inebriated slumber. I jerked upright to find her sitting on the end of my bed, watching me with midnight eyes.

CHAPTER FIVE

I'll not ask how you continually make your entrance into a club where no woman is allowed," I said shakily.

Her answering smile unnerved me. "I am no woman."

I settled my covers nervously over my chest, though I wore both a nightshirt and dressing gown against the cold. The only light in the room was a glow from the nearly spent coals on the hearth, but for some reason, I could see her plainly.

"Well, I am a man who needs sleep." I tried to sound nonchalant, but she disconcerted me in all ways. "Is there a reason for your visit? I stayed home sensibly and engaged in no conversations with were-beasts this evening."

"No, you did not remain home. You visited your lady in St. Martin's Lane." Her tone abruptly softened. "How is she?"

I knew she did not mean Lizzie. "Beautiful. Anne is well and strong."

My lady went silent for a long moment. If she'd been any other person, I'd have thought her weeping, but I had no idea if a night-slayer could shed tears.

"You are good to her," she said, her voice quiet.

"I try to be. Poor lass."

"Why do you care so much about her?" The question held curiosity, as it had when asked by Lizzie.

"I find it strange no one believes it possible I could have sympathy for a child," I answered in some irritation. "My own upbringing was an indifferent one—my older brother received all the attention. Perhaps that's why."

I had no idea myself, except compassion, I supposed, and understanding of Anne's uncertain place in the world.

"I am glad you do," the night-slayer said wistfully then became brisk again. "I had a look at the body."

"Body?" Fog tainted my brain. "You mean Copeland's body?"

She regarded me with those alarming eyes as though I were a simpleton. "He was handsome in life. Rather like you."

Again, I did not know how to answer. Her compliments might be straightforward, or she might mean I'd make a tasty meal.

"How did you manage to see him?" I asked. "Where is he?"

"The Bow Street magistrate's house. In the shed behind it, which is cold enough these days for a body." She sent me one of her dark smiles. "As you've observed, I can get into places I have no business being."

I decided to stop trying to picture how she'd slipped

inside. "What did you conclude? Apart from him being fine looking."

"He was not killed by weres. At least, not obviously."

I sat up straighter. "Why do you say *not obviously*?"

"He died from a knife wound to the throat. Competently done, one deep slice." She demonstrated the slash through the air with alarming precision. "He didn't struggle much, so he must have been taken by surprise. A were-beast would have slashed him quickly, yes, but there would have been more than one cut."

I recalled the razor-sharp claws Seamus's hand had become and agreed. There would be three or four parallel cuts, not a lone one.

"So, Kieran wasn't lying. They didn't do it."

"Oh, I imagine he was lying," the night-slayer said. "Not, perhaps, about Mr. Copeland, but about something. Have a care who you trust, Robert."

"Such as night-slayers who can enter any room they choose."

"Exactly."

I could never have an ordinary conversation with this woman. I wondered if she'd been as cheeky when she'd been alive or whether becoming a night-slayer had altered her character.

"I saw a woman in Bow Street when I emerged," my lady went on. "She was staring up at the house and weeping. Respectable-looking, gown made by a modiste, though not one an aristocrat would frequent, I don't think. A noblewoman wouldn't stand on the street either."

"Copeland's wife?" I hazarded.

"I do not think so, because she had a gentleman with

her, who had his arm around her, trying to coax her home. The woman was too young to be Mr. Copeland's mother, so I suspect a sister, with her husband. They live in Weymouth Street at number 16, just off Portland Place. I followed them, when the gentleman finally persuaded her to take herself indoors."

I drew a breath as I imbibed all this information. "You did not insinuate yourself inside and question them thoroughly?"

"I cannot go *anywhere* I choose, as you believe," she answered in annoyance. "Certain circumstances must be in place. Besides, I would terrify them too much for speech. And I cannot always control my hunger."

I hoped for my sake she was controlling it now. "I was joking. I will speak to them, of course. I wasn't acquainted with Copeland, but I will think of some excuse to visit his family. Perkins said he knew the man slightly. I can always use his name if necessary."

"You were nearby at the time of Copeland's death and are distraught you had not been close enough to prevent it. That is excuse enough."

I adjusted my covers as though they'd be a thick enough barrier to stop her ripping out my heart. "What did I do before I had a night-slayer to do my thinking for me?"

"The Lord only knows." My lady leaned to me, her hand landing slowly on my chest, right over the afore-mentioned heart. "But if you hadn't met me, you'd also be very dead."

True. She'd saved my skin more than once. "I am forever grateful." My words were shaky because her hand was cold, very cold, burning even though the blankets.

"I am forever grateful to *you*, Robert." She lifted her hand away, thankfully. I'd have to check whether its print had seared into my skin. "For your kindness to Anne."

She rose, a picture of gracefulness, her dark green frock falling in modest folds.

"Sleep now," she said.

I couldn't even tighten myself to resist. I crashed to my pillow and slept so hard I did not awaken until the day had progressed almost to noon.

I did not actually bear the mark of her hand on my chest, I saw as I stripped off my dressing gown and night-shirt to don my clothes. But the chill inside it tried to convince me otherwise the rest of the day.

———

NUMBER 16 WEYMOUTH STREET, AROUND THE CORNER from Portland Place, was a respectable enough house, tall and brick, identical to its fellows.

It was not far from where Copeland had been killed, which explained what he'd been doing in that area, either coming or going from his sister's house. Or perhaps he'd lived here as well.

I squared my shoulders, lifted the door knocker, and let it tap-tap-tap on the door.

It was opened by a small young woman in a plain frock and a pinafore, a downstairs maid I guessed. She peered at me from under a plain cap and frizz of brown curls as though startled anyone had come at all.

"Robert Archer, at your service," I said with a bow. "My card." My aristocratic friend Derek Chase had insisted I had calling cards made up, nothing ostentatious, and I held one out to the maid.

She glanced at it, her eyes not registering the letters, but I was not surprised. Many servants couldn't read.

"I'll inquire, sir." The maid gave me a curtsy, let me stand in the foyer out of the cold wind, and disappeared up a flight of gloom-drenched stairs.

She returned not long later—I'd heard male voices above exclaiming *Is it one of the blasted Runners? No? Then who the devil is he?*—and told me to follow her up. I supposed the gentlemen upstairs were willing to satisfy their curiosity by admitting me.

I ascended the dark staircase behind the maid and entered a sitting room that was only marginally better lighted. The winter day hadn't brightened much more than when I'd awoken that morning. A fire danced in the fireplace at least, warming the chamber somewhat, and they'd lit a few candles.

Two men and a woman stood in the middle of the well-furnished room, all three regarding me in consternation. The woman must be the one my night-slayer had seen in Bow Street, as her eyes were red-rimmed, her nose swollen from incessant weeping.

The gentleman hovering protectively next to her was likely her husband. The second man, flanking the husband's other side, wore a well-tailored suit with slim trousers and had his fair hair artfully curled on the top of his head.

"Mr. Archer?" the husband asked uncertainly.

I bowed. "I have come to offer you my condolences, madam, on the death of your brother."

The woman's interest rose the slightest bit. "Oh. Did you know James?"

"I regret not." I repeated my night-slayer's suggested story that I'd been nearby when his murder happened and was devastated I hadn't stopped it. "I am truly sorry, madam." I was, indeed, as her eyes brimmed with fresh tears. This poor lady was honestly grieving.

"Not your fault," her husband said to me. "I am Stephen Jacobs, and this is my wife, James's sister, Gemma."

"Pleased to make your acquaintance," I responded dutifully.

"You are an army man, your card indicates," Jacobs said. "As was I. The Seventeenth Foot."

"Twenty-Sixth Rifles," I answered. "In the thick of things at Waterloo, as were you. Brave men in the Seventeenth. You barely made it out, from what I heard."

"It was a close-run thing," Jacobs acknowledged.

"Phillip Lanham." The dandy interrupted us, vexed he couldn't join in the exchange between veterans. "James's dearest friend. I know of you, Archer. I am acquainted with Mr. Chase."

Many people claimed acquaintanceship with Chase. He was obnoxiously wealthy and also humble, which made people, including myself, like to be near him.

"I will greet him for you when I see him again," I said. "Now, madam, is there anything I can do for you during this terrible time? Speak with the Runners, or anyone else, on your behalf? You do not need to be bothered when you only wish to mourn your brother."

"They will not release James to us." Gemma lifted a handkerchief and mopped her nose with it. Her husband stepped even closer, while Lanham looked as though he'd like to be the one at her side.

"They are waiting for the inquest," I said. Mr. Perkins had related this to me before he'd departed the club. He'd not known much more than that. "To bring a verdict about his death. That should happen in the next day or so, and then Mr. Copeland can be decently interred."

Gemma gave me a grateful nod, though Lanham was obviously not convinced. "There's no need for such intricacy," he growled. "Everyone knows those weres did it. Insatiable louts."

I decided not to share my theory that the insatiable louts had not committed this crime. It would not comfort Gemma and only alert Lanham and Jacobs that I was poking for information.

Jacobs broke in. "Even so, Lanham, we need to wait for the law to go through its paces."

Lanham snorted, but Gemma said, "Peace, Mr. Lanham. He is right. Mr. Archer is only trying to console us."

Lanham broke off his derisive noises. "Your pardon, Gems."

Interesting that Lanham not only addressed her by her Christian name but gave her a pet name at that. This told me they'd been acquainted for a very long time, perhaps from childhood. I could tell that Gemma's husband did not like this suggestion of intimacy, but Jacobs schooled his expression.

"I suppose the poor fellow was walking home from a New Year's revelry," I said. "As was I. Did he live here with you?"

Gemma nodded sadly. "He'd gone to a gathering at a club. The Wakefield in Gower Street. He leased this house. We lived here with him."

The Wakefield was a few doors down from my regimental club. I hadn't known Copeland had been so close.

He must have been a generous fellow to allow his sister and her husband to share the house with him. Either Jacobs didn't have much blunt, or they were all economizing together. I wondered if Copeland's will and lease arrangement would let them stay now.

I also wondered how much Lanham would hover over them. Had he been close to Copeland, or to Gemma?

"Well, I am truly sorry your New Year's celebrations were so tragically curtailed," I said.

Gemma sent me a half-smile. "Stephen and I had been spending the evening quietly at home."

"Copeland had asked me to join him," Jacobs put in quickly. "But I did not want to leave Gemma on her own."

Lanham looked displeased, as though he'd been counting on Jacobs being out of the way that night. "I was celebrating at my own club, in St. James's." Lanham stressed the location, a club there being superior, in his view, to anything in Gower Street.

"I regret that none of us were with him," I said. "If I'd only been a street closer …"

"You couldn't have fought off weres," Lanham said

with a sneer. "Not even if you were in the acclaimed rifles."

I shrugged, as though humbled by his reminder. "That is so. Well, I will detain you no longer. But please call upon me or send word if I can be of any service. I'm in Gower Street myself, at the army club there."

"Near Copeland's," Lanham rushed to point out. "Funny you say you didn't know him."

Now he was giving me suspicious glares, as though he suspected me of pushing Copeland into a pack of weres and fleeing.

"I don't know many outside my regiment," I explained. "Mr. Copeland wasn't an army man." I'd only guessed this but Jacobs confirmed it.

"He was not." Jacobs shook his head. "It isn't odd, Lanham. Everyone has a set, including you."

"True." Lanham both grudgingly conceded and managed to look superior at the same time. I'd already decided I did not like the chap.

I bowed once more, directing my words to Gemma. "You do have my deepest sympathies, madam. Again, please send word if I can assist you."

I included the gentlemen in my farewell nod and told them I'd see myself out. The little maid popped out of nowhere to escort me, and I was certain she'd heard every word of the conversation.

Downstairs, the maid shut the front door behind me, and I stepped into wind that had grown icier. I turned up the collar of my greatcoat, pressed down my hat, and walked into it, making for the warmth of my club.

I pondered on the problem as I went. I'd hoped to

uncover a murderer in that house, whose guilt would have him confessing on his knees before me. Instead, I'd found a bewildered sister, a watchful husband, and a disagreeable friend, each nervous in their own way.

Had Copeland been sent to his grave by the sympathetic husband who didn't appear to have shed a tear? Jacobs's eyes had been dry and bright, though his worry about his wife had not been feigned.

Or had the close friend, who was annoyed with the slowness of the law, done the deed? Once the weres were pronounced as the culprits, no one would look closely at Lanham, would they?

I wondered if Copeland had noticed Lanham's obvious interest in his married sister. If Copeland had confronted Lanham and threatened to tell Gemma's husband about his lecherousness, perhaps Lanham had silenced Copeland.

Or would Lanham have tried to off Jacobs, instead? Then Lanham could be the one comforting Gemma.

Then again, perhaps Jacobs had quarreled with his brother-in-law and struck out in anger. According to my night-slayer, Copeland hadn't struggled and must have been taken by surprise. One cut to the throat, and he was done.

Copeland wouldn't have run or fought if his brother-in-law had joined him on the walk home. In fact, he'd have welcomed the company in the darkness. As Copeland had invited Jacobs to the club and its New Year's festivities, he wouldn't be surprised if he ran across Jacobs somewhere nearby.

Jacobs could have distracted him and competently cut his throat. As an army man, he'd know how.

The Seventeenth Foot had been up against it at Waterloo, nearly surrounded and cut off from the rest of the army. They'd fought their way back inch by inch, an ordeal that would have hardened any man.

Of course, it would be worth checking to discover whether Lanham had been at *his* club in St. James's at all that night, as he'd claimed.

Even as I mused, I was aware of quiet footfalls behind me, keeping perfect pace with mine.

In the shadows of Howland Street, the very place James Copeland had met his end, I spun to confront my stalker.

"No need to lurk," I informed the deeper shadow that had stepped into a doorway. "Please tell Kieran I am doing all I can."

CHAPTER SIX

Seamus, the man with the golden eyes of a wolf, stepped into the lane to face me.

"For your protection, he says," Seamus grunted. I assumed he meant that Kieran had sent him. "Even if you have a tame night-slayer."

I gave him a tight smile. "I told you before, she isn't tame."

I was pleased to see Seamus shoot a nervous glance behind him, though my lady was nowhere in sight.

"Well then." I settled my hat against a gust of wind and courageously turned my back on Seamus. "Shall we walk?"

"What were you doing in that house?" Seamus was next to me before I saw him move. I pretended that didn't alarm me.

"Trying to find out who murdered Copeland," I answered, keeping my voice steady. "It's in your best interest that I do, you know."

"By talking to people?" His tone was incredulous.

"Yes." I glanced at him in curiosity. "What would you do? Rush about searching for a scent?"

"I would, if it weren't so dangerous. Too many people in this part of London."

"Kieran took me to Whitechapel," I reminded him. "Its inhabitants live cheek-by-jowl."

"They're used to weres." Seamus flipped a hand to indicate the brick houses around us. "Here, they pretend we don't exist."

I had to concede his point. "Easier to live that way," I said. "No one wants to look over his shoulder every day, fearing he'll be torn to shreds at any step."

"You might be anyway." Seamus's growl told me that while Kieran might trust me somewhat, Seamus did not. "Or clouted by a human footpad for the coat off your back."

"True. But I was in the army. I know how to fight."

Seamus's growl became a snarl. "Gods, the arrogance of you. I should take you out now and save Kieran the trouble."

Sweat beaded on my brow despite the wind. Seamus could slay me quickly with those claws of his, and I'd be found in a pool of blood, another victim of London's streets. There was no one in this narrow lane at the moment, and its many windows were shuttered against the cold. Would anyone come to my aid against a were?

"I mean Kieran no harm," I said hastily. "I said I'd help, and I will." I peered at him. "What were you three doing in this part of town on New Year's Eve, anyway? If you're more welcome in Whitechapel, why come to Bloomsbury?"

"None of your affair." Seamus's hands curled in his gloves, and I imagined his claws emerging.

"I certainly don't need to know all your secrets," I assured him. "I wouldn't want to know them. But you must see it's a strange coincidence that you were far outside your territory at the same time a gentleman of this area was murdered. I've discovered that he was killed with a knife, not claws or teeth, but you could have used a weapon as a diversion."

"Better shut your gob, army man."

I studied Seamus and the rage in his eyes. He could have done the murder, with or without Kieran's knowledge, as a protective measure. My dry mouth encouraged me in this belief.

"I am only trying to put forth arguments that someone might in court," I said, trying to soothe him. "You must see it looks very bad."

Between one step and the next, I suddenly had a very strong hand around my throat. Seamus lifted me casually into the air and slammed me against the nearest wall, holding me there. My head thumped on the hard stone, and my hat fell to the pavement.

"Not for you to question us," Seamus snarled. "You find the killer, or you die."

I gasped for breath and found none. I couldn't argue while I was being strangled, so I satisfied myself with trying to pry away his hand.

I failed. I felt the claws through the thin leather of his gloves, which any moment would slice through the fabric into my throat.

Seamus's breath held a hint of liquor but he was

perfectly sober. His eyes, though, bore rage, hatred, and a touch of madness.

"Better, I break your neck now, before you betray us."

I kicked hard, trying to catch him in the balls, but Seamus easily blocked me with a powerful thigh. I would die here in this lane, as Copeland had done, without a friend to assist him.

Seamus squeezed. My vision went black as I in vain tried to twist from his grasp.

Was my final thought regret I was at such odds with my brother? Or concern for the children I wanted to look after?

No, it was wonder that the army and navy refused to use weres to help fight their battles. Not honorable, they'd concluded. Fools. Weres would send a human army running without a shot fired.

With a suddenness that had me collapsing to the ground, Seamus was yanked away from me. He sailed across the narrow street and crashed into the bricks opposite.

Instantly, he was on his feet, barely winded, but a slim and fiercely strong hand grabbed me under the arm and hauled me up.

I was never certain what happened after that. The lane swirled around me, faster and faster, bricks and windows blurring. Lights flickered in a constant whirl as they had when I'd danced at New Year's, but the air rushing past me was brutally cold.

When my night-slayer steadied me on my feet again, I was standing in my own small bedchamber at my club, the floor solid beneath me. A flame of my coal fire flared up, cutting the chill.

She released me, but my head still spun, and my roiling stomach protested. I barely made it to my empty slop pail, where I spilled what little I had eaten that day into it.

I rinsed my mouth and hands in clean water in the basin and turned to the night-slayer, drying myself shakily with my thin towel.

"What the devil was that?" I asked when I could finally speak.

My night-slayer today was dressed in a dark maroon frock, very fetching, with every seam in place.

"I can move quickly when I wish to." Her hair wasn't mussed, either. "I decided I'd better get you away from Seamus."

Her explanation accounted for the chill wind I felt whenever she suddenly appeared. If she could move that swiftly, she'd bring a draft with her.

"I am grateful," I said sincerely. "How did you know I'd be able to move along with you?"

"I didn't." She shrugged in the manner that told me she'd left human compassion behind long ago. "But it does not matter. You are here now. Why did you provoke him?"

"Not my intention to." I finished wiping my hands and discarded the towel. Oddly, I still wore my greatcoat and hat, and I slid them off as I spoke, the mundane action calming me a little. "It occurred to me that one of the weres *could* have done it, using a human weapon as a blind."

"Possibly, but I doubt they'd have insisted on your help

in that case." She moved to my bed, sat without awkwardness on its edge, lifted my notebook from my night table, and began leafing through it, reading my private thoughts.

"I was thinking Seamus or the other were—Ross— might have killed Copeland without Kieran being the wiser," I said.

"I doubt it. He's their leader, and he'd know. Wolves in a pack can discern what one another does. By scent, or something." She dismissed this oddity with a flick of her fingers as she scanned the pages. "These are your notes on the case?"

"Not much there. I've only just spoken to Copeland's family—and friend." Lanham was my favorite suspect, though I'd have to find proof of his guilt.

"You have organized things well," she said with approval. I'd listed the few people I'd spoken to—Perkins, Kieran—and what they'd said, marking what I thought was significant versus the trivial.

I sank to the chair near the fire, still trying to find my breath. "Habit from my army days. I had to keep track of my men and who needed what."

"I thought sergeants did that."

Most ladies I met had only the vaguest idea of ranks in the army, other than the higher officers. It made me wonder again about her history.

"Sergeants take care of logistics, but a good officer needs to know the strengths and weaknesses of his men, who can be counted on in a crisis, and who should be kept to the rear. I was Rifles, so I had to know where to position the best shooters and how to use rivalries between the marksmen to my advantage."

"You miss it," she observed.

I shrugged, my whole body longing for a brandy. "It was a time in my life I could be myself, without living in Freddy's shadow or being lambasted by him for every fault."

"Would you go back?"

"No." I stretched my feet toward the fire. "I'm too soft now. I prefer sleeping in a bed instead of on a cot or the ground, and I like having my coals replenished every morning."

"You are a liar." She pinned me with her dark gaze, then went back to my notes. "What did you think of the family?"

I did not like that she read me so easily. I proceeded to summarize the visit to Copeland's house as succinctly as I could.

"The sister is genuinely sorry Copeland is gone," I concluded. "The gentlemen are not. Phillip Lanham claimed, rather nervously, that he was at his club all night. I can check that. I have a friend who frequents the most prestigious clubs of St. James's. He either will have seen Lanham or can ask if others did."

"The sister and her husband will vouch for each other, which does not guarantee the husband's innocence," she said.

"I know." I heaved a sigh. "I suppose I should quiz the maid and anyone who worked in or around their house on the night to find out if Jacobs left it."

"The sister herself might have done it," my lady pointed out. "There were those who shed tears for me, hiding their joy that I was gone."

I regarded her in shock. Had she attended her own funeral? That was both macabre and sad.

She smiled. "Imagine how satisfying it was to greet them again."

"I don't wish to." I suppressed a shudder. "Your anecdotes are not comforting, my lady."

"They're not meant to be. I am making the point that you should not disregard Copeland's sister because you feel sorry for her."

"I hope it's Lanham." I drew a breath, forcing myself to focus on the question at hand. "He's a nasty piece of work if ever I saw one."

"Do not let your perceptions shield you from the truth. Each of these people are equally possible as murderers. Even if the sister did not ply the knife herself, she could have hired or coerced someone to do it for her."

I lifted my hands. "I will be diligent and go through it all again. What I have not decided is why Kieran and his mates were lingering in the area at all. Seamus made it plain that they don't like to stray out of territories where they're tolerated. With good reason. At the first sign of trouble, everyone points to the supernatural in the wrong place at the wrong time."

My lady's brows rose. "You sound like an enlightened gentleman."

"Not really. Earlier in my life I regarded supernaturals as ravenous killers that should be hunted down the moment they were seen. I've been forced to change my ideas."

She responded with a little smile. "I will take that as a compliment. As to why the were-beasts were nearby, they were visiting someone in Queen Anne Street. I had a look in the house today. A gentleman lives there who is purporting to be an ordinary human, but the whiff of were-beast on him is unmistakable."

I sat up straight. "A were? Living in Queen Anne Street? Well, good God, maybe *he's* our killer. How on earth did a were manage to let rooms in this part of London?"

Her stare turned derisive. "I take back my observation that you are an enlightened gentleman. *At the first sign of trouble, everyone points to the supernatural in the wrong place at the wrong time.*"

"Yes, all right, I am an idiot." I tried to calm my alarm and return to logic. "If Kieran and his mates were visiting him at the time, and they were all inside the house, then no, none of them would have been out murdering Copeland. But we can't put aside the possibility. Maybe Kieran found this were standing over Copeland's body and hustled him indoors."

"The man letting rooms in the house very carefully conceals his were-beast state," my lady stated. "He might be half-were, half-human, which puts him in a precarious position. I didn't speak to him, only observed him, but he tries very hard to suppress his animal nature. I will guess that Kieran did not go there for a friendly visit. The weres hold allegiance to a group very highly. This man might be part of Kieran's pack, and Kieran went either to check on his welfare or try to bring him back into the fold."

"Any inquiry I make in that direction will be danger-ous." I gingerly touched my throat, where Seamus had gripped it. "I suppose they are trying to protect their own."

"They prefer to deal with any transgressions themselves. If this half-were *had* killed Mr. Copeland, I imagine Kieran would have taken him far from the area, by force if necessary. They wouldn't have wanted the Runners associating weres with the death."

"Then the fact that the Runners do suspect them points to their innocence," I offered. "They wouldn't have stayed to be found, which means they had no idea the murder was taking place a few streets away. Their bad luck that someone stumbled over the body around the same time I was struggling to get away from them."

I frowned. Who *had* found Copeland when three weres were so conveniently nearby? Or had the coincidence simply been the murderer's good fortune?

"I will have to speak to Kieran again," I decided.

"He will not want to admit he'd gone to visit the half-were," my lady said. "You must assure him you will keep your silence on it. You have been asked to prove their innocence, and he will have to cooperate with you."

I briefly glanced heavenward. "You make it sound so simple."

My lady set aside my notebook and rose. "It *is* simple. You complicate matters, Robert. You should rest now and then continue your pursuit."

I pointed a finger at her as my eyelids abruptly drooped. "You must cease doing *that*. How do I know what you're getting up to when you send me to sleep?"

"It was a suggestion in this instance," she said with impatience. "Moving as we did exhausts a human. What I get up to when you are slumbering is making certain you don't fall out of your bed or choke on whatever you might disgorge. You think highly of yourself if you believe anything else."

I flushed. "I didn't mean *that*." I admired ladies, yes, and enjoyed my bit of pleasure, but I was a rather modest man. "I meant sampling a bit of my blood."

She was in front of me in a flash, leaning over me in that alarming fashion, her breath cold on my face. "I never have. If I started on you, Robert, I would drain you before I could cease."

With that disturbing announcement, she stepped back and vanished. The freezing draft in her wake told me she'd departed in that awful speed that had made me ill.

I was almost ill again, but I bravely held myself together. I let out a long breath once the fire restored the room to some warmth, then took her advice and stretched myself out on the bed and had a much-needed rest. It was dark outside by the time I'd recovered.

I WROTE TO DEREK CHASE WHEN I ROSE, ASKING HIM about Lanham and clubs on New Year's Eve. I also penned a note to Perkins, telling him I'd met Copeland's family and asking for a bit more about them if he knew anything, since he'd been acquainted with Copeland.

I took the letters downstairs for the concierge to post and hailed a hackney for Whitechapel.

The inhabitants of the tavern there were mildly surprised to see me when I entered but said nothing as I took a seat and ordered ale and another helping of their splendid beefsteak.

Kieran arrived not long later, accompanied only by Ross. I craned to search for Seamus, but if he was nearby, he was keeping out of sight.

I hadn't sent for Kieran or asked to meet him, but I guessed rightly that word would go out that I'd returned to the tavern. Kieran took the seat across from me, while red-haired Ross sat next to me and watched my every move.

Kieran's face went stony as I revealed that I knew about the half-were gentleman who lived in Queen Anne's Lane.

I took a nonchalant sip of ale when I finished my confession. "If you give me your word he didn't kill Copeland, and you aren't covering up for him, then I promise, I will say nothing and resume my task."

Before Kieran could answer, Ross rumbled derisively. "We'd never defend him."

Kieran shot him a quelling glance, and Ross subsided, suddenly focusing on his ale.

"Since you already know," Kieran growled, "I will tell you I was trying to persuade him back to Whitechapel, where he belongs. His people are here, but he insists—" He broke off. "That is not your worry. We were with him for an hour and more, and he rarely goes out at all. If he'd murdered that gentleman, we'd know."

I had little doubt they would. "Were you aware of the murder at all? Before there was a hue and cry?"

"No." Kieran spoke emphatically. "We didn't know until the Runner from the Whitechapel house, an arrogant cur who believes he's not afraid of us, came to question me. I thought you had betrayed our presence in that part of the city, but my sources told me that wasn't so."

I briefly wondered who these sources were but knew any questions would be futile.

"Your Runner obviously couldn't say for certain that you were the culprit," I remarked. "You're still at liberty, and not languishing in the prison in Southwark."

"Not a prison," Kieran said grimly. "A filthy hulk with enchantments woven through to keep us confined."

I recoiled. The night-slayer had mentioned a place worse than Newgate, but she hadn't been specific. I'd seen the hulks, menacing ships with no masts or keels, dredged into mud, where prisoners languished. Most of the condemned awaited transport across the seas to a life of hard labor, and few were reprieved. The stench of the ships was enough to keep the curious at a distance.

The hulks for humans were bad enough—I could imagine what measures were taken against weres.

"I will endeavor to keep you free," I said. "Copeland should have justice, not simply vengeance."

"I thought you didn't know Mr. Copeland," Kieran said.

"Never met the man. But if I'd taken a different route that night, the chap lying dead in the street might have been me."

As I said this, it struck me that I'd been looking at this situation the wrong way around. I adjusted my thoughts, and when I did, new and astonishing possibilities came into my head.

I shoveled the last of the roast into my mouth and

followed it with a swallow of ale. "I must be off." I rose without waiting for Kieran to dismiss me. "I have a few people to speak to before I'm certain you'll be safe."

Kieran put himself in front of me before I took a step. He couldn't move as fast as my lady night-slayer, but he was plenty swift. Ross closed behind me, his body heat ominous against my back.

"You will say *nothing* about the man in Queen Anne Street," Kieran stated in a low growl.

I huffed, offended. "I gave you my promise."

Kieran leaned closer. "Many a gentleman don't consider their promises to a were to be binding. Know that if you break yours, not only will you suffer, but your family will as well. As I said, we know who they are and where they are."

My heartbeat sped both in worry and irritation. "I keep my word to everyone. I have that much honor, at least. If you want to have a go at Freddy for my good behavior, do. I might enjoy it. However." I frowned sternly up at him, trying to be as menacing as he. "You let Margery and her son be. They are not to be touched, for any reason. Nor are any of my friends. You will regret it greatly if you do."

I meant that if he sought out Lizzie and Jack, my lady would strenuously object to Kieran and his seconds anywhere near her daughter. Were-beasts were tough and very dangerous, but they'd be no match for a furious night-slayer.

I also reflected that while I'd returned from the war with nothing, I now had three children whose welfare I cared about. That thought filled me with both joy and dread.

"Keep your word, and neither of us have anything to fear," Kieran said.

"I'm glad we understand each other." I took up my hat. "I will endeavor to solve this problem quickly so that I might be finished with you. Though this tavern is a fine one. I shall miss it."

Kieran smiled at me, but his expression was disquieting. "Return any time you wish. I have told the proprietor to always admit you." Ross, the man of few words, chuckled behind me.

A standing invitation to the beast's lair. I would have to regretfully decline. Even with the excellence of the beefsteak, the price for enjoying it might be too high.

I managed to give Kieran a dignified nod and sidestep him, pulling my greatcoat closer and clapping on my hat as I stepped out into the winter evening, breathing a sigh of relief.

When I returned to the club, I had answers to both my letters, which clarified a few things.

I read the letters through again, going over them with my new idea in mind. I thought I was correct with my guess, and if I was, that solution made me very, very angry.

CHAPTER SEVEN

Late the next morning, I met Almay at our favorite tavern in Tottenham Court Road. We often dined here or simply came for coffee or ale, away from the mediocre fare served to us at our club. The food in this place was a far cry from that in the Whitechapel tavern, but it would have to do.

Before we'd done more than sip at our ale, Derek Chase joined us.

"Good morning, all," he said in his dandified drawl. "Frightfully early, isn't it?"

"Agreed," I said. "Almay was up with the lark, riding his steed through Regent's Park."

Derek shuddered. "You army fellows are insane." He took the third chair at our table, one left empty, and nodded for the barmaid to bring him ale.

Derek's suit was natty as usual, though he'd likely not bothered to dress as carefully as he would if meeting with his peers at Brooks's. The three of us had long been friends and didn't stand on formality. That meant Derek's cravat was tied in only a slightly complicated knot, and his pristine greatcoat and boots actually bore one or two specks of dust.

"I have often told Almay so," I said to Derek as his ale arrived. "I gave up my army ways and became the slovenly fellow I used to be. Now then. Phillip Lanham?"

"An oik," Derek pronounced after a hearty sip. "Tries to mingle with the highest born he can and pretend he is one of them. I am not surprised he is after the dead chap's sister if she is comely. He has an eye for the ladies."

"She is pretty," I confirmed. "But also devoted to her husband, and he to her, if I read the signs correctly."

"Even so, I'd tell the husband to look out," Derek said. "However, Lanham was at his club on New Year's Eve at the time you mention, as I told you in my note. I saw him. Lost himself in deep play and was still at it at three in the morning. I took a hundred guineas off him, the idiot."

I scowled across the table at the empty seat. "I hoped I was wrong and that it was Lanham. He needs to be taken down a peg or two."

"I agree." Derek shrugged. "He will have to dig his own grave another way, which he will, I'm certain."

"Small comfort." I sighed.

I'd written my thoughts into my notebook last night, just in case, and left it in plain sight on my night table. My hope was that if I didn't return this morning, either the charlady or the concierge would grow curious and read it. Or my lady night-slayer might find it and make certain she dropped it into the correct hands.

"Ah." Almay glanced across the tavern and lifted his hand.

Mr. Perkins, whom I'd asked Almay to invite as well, greeted us and slid into the waiting chair.

I introduced him to Derek. Perkins admitted knowing him by reputation and seemed a bit in awe of someone so famous in the *ton*.

After the two greeted each other and more ale was fetched, I turned to my purpose.

"I am sorry to bother you, Perkins. Your letter was enlightening, but I have a few more questions about Copeland, if you don't mind."

Perkins nodded good-naturedly. "Fire away."

"How did you find out about Copeland's death in the first place? You told Almay about it that morning. Chase and I agree that Almay rises appallingly early, but you must have been up before he was. Or, you found out about the murder the night before, shortly after it occurred. Do you recall which?"

Perkins looked confused a moment, then his expression cleared. "My clerk told me. Sent word very early, yes. He hangs about Bow Street in the mornings, drumming up business for our chambers. He learns who was brought in overnight and listens to their morning hearings. He's awake even before you, Almay."

Derek sent Perkins an amazed look. "I'd not believed that was possible."

"I thought solicitors brought you your cases," I said, ignoring Derek's attempt at humor. "Either for prosecution or defense."

"They do." Perkins nodded. "But our clerk finds the juiciest ones and sends them to the solicitors we work with. The brief is then given to us."

"Your clerk told you of Copeland's murder, and you hoped to get in at the starting post, so to speak," I said.

"Exactly." Perkins lifted his ale. "Also, Copeland was an acquaintance, and I was distressed for his family."

Perkins had replied to my request for more information about Gemma and her husband with a few details, but he'd admitted he'd not known much about Jacobs and nothing at all about Lanham.

I was sweet on Copeland's sister for a time, years ago, he'd written, *though she did not reciprocate. She married Jacobs after I'd lost touch with the family. Copeland had never been happy about anyone with interest in Gemma, but Jacobs was very persistent, I believe. Adamantly so. I suppose he wore Copeland down after a time.*

"You mentioned in your letter that it was Copeland's idea his sister and husband lived with him," I said.

Perkins set down his tankard. "That is what I have heard. Copeland was always very protective of Gemma. Jacobs won her hand but I suppose Copeland had the final victory of keeping her close."

"And now he's gone," Almay pointed out.

"Will they stay in the house?" I asked. "I wondered if the lease extended to the whole family, or if they will have to vacate it now that Copeland is dead."

Perkins shook his head. "I have no idea. It would depend on how the lease was written. I suppose I could find out, if it's important."

"Possibly." Was Jacobs relieved that his overbearing brother-in-law would no longer bother them? Or unhappy because they'd be turned out of decent lodgings?

"I'll ask my clerk." Perkins took another sip of ale. "He's a mine of information."

"Speaking of your clerk," I went on, "how did he know the Runners wanted to blame were-beasts for Copeland's murder? More eavesdropping? Come to think of it, how did anyone know there were were-beasts in the area at all? They are fairly secretive."

"You do ask devilishly tricky questions," Perkins said with a grin. "Are you sure you didn't train to blather in court for a living? Of course it was known the weres had been there. You saw them."

"But I told no one," I said. "I rushed home when I escaped them and slept off both my fright and the large amount of brandy and champagne I'd consumed. I learned that the weres had been accused only when Almay revealed this to me the next morning. So, others must have known before that."

Perkins shrugged. "I suppose."

I was momentarily distracted by a young woman who passed through the outer hall on the way to the snug, her downcast face concealed by a velvet bonnet. She did not look up, and no one else took note of her before she vanished from sight.

"Copeland wasn't murdered by the weres," I said, resuming my narrative. "Which I hope I have already established. He was killed by a man with a knife, with one slash across the throat. A wiser man would have made several slashes, to feign a were's claws. But the murderer likely wasn't thinking very clearly, having decided to kill Copeland on the spur of the moment." I shook my head. "Poor fellow. Copeland had done nothing but walk through the wrong street at the wrong time. If I'd left the New Year's ball I'd attended any earlier, the killer might have chosen *me*."

"You, Archer?" Derek asked in bewilderment. "Why would anyone want to murder you? Anyone apart from your dear brother, I mean."

"No one." I let my tone grow severe. "That is my point. Copeland was simply convenient. If Lanham had decided to commit murder, I suspect he'd have chosen to rid Gemma of her husband, instead. Copeland was protective, Perkins says, but Lanham in his arrogance might have believed Copeland would welcome him, since they were old friends. Lanham, however, strikes me as a coward, and also you can vouch for him at the time in question, Chase. But what about your clerk?" I asked Perkins.

Perkins blinked. "What I about him? Not following you, I'm afraid."

"He tries to bring you cases that will make your name, correct? Perhaps he was wandering about New Year's Eve and noted the weres nearby. Perhaps he decided that a murder by weres would be worth taking on. If you prosecuted, you'd be lauded for saving London from the menace of brutal were-beasts. If you defended, as the were-beasts have asked you to, and won, you'd be considered a genius, as you yourself speculated. Perhaps your clerk decided to help things along."

"Good Lord." Perkins stared at me in distress, while Almay and Derek looked as shocked. "He is very devoted to us—mostly because he receives a percentage of our fees. The more prominent the cases, the more blunt we can hope to make, which trickles down to him. But good God, that he'd stoop to murder …" Perkins shook his head. "I shall have to report this, I suppose, and have him arrested. A pity. He's a rather good clerk."

I sat back, giving the semblance of a relaxed man, but my hands on the table were tight. "You swallowed that rather easily," I said.

Perkins's brow wrinkled. "I beg your pardon?"

"Do you give this much credence to every statement laid before you?" I asked. "You cannot be much of a barrister if you do."

His perplexity grew. "I'm sorry, Archer, but you've lost me."

By Almay's and Derek's expressions, I'd lost them as well, though Almay started to understand.

"James Copeland was murdered for no other reason than he was walking through Howland Street on his way home from a New Year's celebration," I said. "On any other night, he'd have been in no danger, but on New Year's Eve, at that precise time, there happened to be three were-beasts in the area, who were spotted by our killer. What a golden opportunity to murder Copeland and lay the blame at their feet."

"So you've said," Perkins said. "But *not* by my clerk?"

"No." I held his gaze. "That should relieve you, he being such a good clerk and all."

"It does." Perkins's face was strained. "I assure you."

"No, it does not relieve you," I said. "Because if I don't truly believe the clerk is guilty, then I need to put the blame on someone else. You, for instance."

"*Me?*" Perkins pointed to himself in astonishment.

"Where were you New Year's Eve?" I asked. "At a revelry? Something in your chambers, perhaps?"

"No." The answer came from Almay, who sounded a bit sickly. "He was with me, at our club, as my guest. He'd gone off not long after midnight."

"And went home, dash it," Perkins said.

"You live in Oxford Street," Almay went on. "So, you'd have crossed Tottenham Court Road, as you always do."

Perkins's face darkened. "This is absolute rot."

"How would you *not* have known about the murder that night?" I demanded. "If you were walking, say, to Portland Street? You'd have heard the commotion when Copeland was found, if you hadn't stumbled across him yourself. Yet you contend you had no idea until your clerk told you about it in the morning."

"You had no idea either," Perkins shot back.

That was true, and I had to think swiftly to counter his remark. "I was farther from Copeland than you were, and I have three were-beasts to give me an alibi. At the moment, they were having a bloody good try at pounding me senseless." I laughed without mirth. "But for my great good luck, there'd have been a trial for *my* murder, and Copeland would be free for his sister to dote upon."

"Mr. Chase, are you accepting this?" Perkins asked Derek in outrage. Derek admonishing me would hold some weight with polite society and save Perkins's reputation.

"Let him speak," Derek said in the tone that few argued with.

"You told me yourself that you were acquainted with Copeland," I resumed. "Copeland likely thought nothing of it when you came upon him on the street and offered to walk with him. It was dark, New Year's Eve can be dangerous, and two gentlemen together would be safer than on their own. You might have been exhilarated by having escaped the weres' notice, and also reminded how Copeland had ruined your suit with his sister."

"I told you, she did not reciprocate my feelings," Perkins all but snarled. "I let her be."

"Perhaps Copeland encouraged her to reject you. Or, at least, you believe that of him, or you'd not have mentioned that fact of his character. Not only did you have the chance to shove the blame onto supernatural beings no one trusts but take out your frustration on the man who thwarted your happiness years before." I made a conceding gesture. "I am speculating, I confess, on this motivation. I believe you'd have continued resenting him in silence if the opportunity to murder him hadn't presented itself so neatly."

Perkins glared as I ran through this speech. "Why shouldn't we believe *you* murdered Copeland?" he demanded. "I wager you're inventing this fight with the were-beasts. No matter how good an army man you were, you'd never stand a chance against three of them, especially as one was a pack guard. *They* are truly vicious."

My brows rose. "How did you know one was a pack guard? I only told you about the one who sought me out. I never gave you any details about the other two. In any case, I'd never heard the term before this moment."

Perkins flushed a dull red. "Stands to reason. No pack leader would travel about London without his guard."

"I didn't give you *that* detail, either," I said. "In fact, I didn't know Kieran was a pack leader."

"My clerk knew." Perkins's voice rose. "The Runners would have said—"

"I think that is enough." Derek broke in with the firm, authoritative voice all upper-class gentlemen were trained to use from boyhood. "Hadn't you better confess, Perkins, and get it over with?"

"You believe him?" Perkins asked incredulously.

"As do I," Almay said. "Damnation, Perkins. I offered to see you all the way to Oxford Street to make certain you'd be safe. If I had, you might have decided *I'd* do as a victim, or else you'd have dragged *me* into your crime. This isn't the first time you've done something spurious to land a court case, though I never thought you'd stoop to murder."

Perkins might have bluffed it out and walked away. After all, I had no evidence, only my guesses and the conflicting story he'd told.

But Perkins lost his temper. "Damn you, Archer." He leapt to his feet, a hardness in his eyes banishing all ingenuousness. "I'll have the lot of you for slander." He rounded on Almay, who'd risen to block his way from the room. "Sit down, Almay. I'll cut you, I swear it."

A knife blade gleamed in his hand. Perkins held it competently, and Almay stepped out of his way. Perkins bathed us in a final glare before he strode past Almay and out of the tavern.

We pursued him, of course. Almay and I rapidly followed Perkins out the door, though Derek stopped to speak to a hefty man who'd been seated in the inglenook.

Perkins lay in wait for us in the next lane. Again, he'd have likely been all right if he'd simply gone home, because even if I told a magistrate my tale, I had nothing but conjecture to offer. I suppose Perkins couldn't take that chance.

He attacked Almay first, rightly perceiving he was the better fighter and should be taken care of right away. Perkins proved competent with the knife, and Almay cursed when the blade met his flesh. Almay danced out of the way of more strikes, and I tried to grab Perkins and relieve him of the knife.

Perkins twisted, waving his blade too close to my gut. I lunged around it, but he evaded me and finally decided to run.

"No," Almay called to me, holding a wounded arm as I started after him. "Let him go."

I ignored him and raced behind Perkins. My goal was no longer to defeat him, but to save his life.

I rounded a corner into a still smaller lane and found Perkins hanging in the grip of a slim young woman who held him several feet off the ground with her hand around his throat.

"Stop," I told her sternly.

My night-slayer had never listened to me, and she didn't now. She squeezed harder, and Perkins gasped for breath and clawed at her hands, much as I had done with Seamus.

"Confess your sins," she hissed at him. "And I'll forget I'm hungry."

She loosened her grip just enough for Perkins to let out a wail. "All right, all right. I did it. Just as Archer said. I killed Copeland to pin it on the weres. For God's sake, man, make her leave me be."

He pleaded as though I had any control over a night-slayer.

Heavy footsteps sounded behind me. I turned as Derek and the large man from the tavern sped into the lane, followed by a half-stumbling Almay. Almay was enraged, blood dripping from his slashed arm.

I swung back around, fearing the night-slayer, smelling Almay's blood, would attack him, but I found her gone. Perkins knelt in the lane alone, weeping in fear, a red welt on his throat.

"Now then, Mr. Perkins," the large man said. "I'm Mr. Hawthorne, a Runner from Bow Street. I heard your confession, sir, and an interesting one it was. Shall we be off to speak to the magistrate?"

———

"WHAT THE DEVIL DID YOU SAY TO HIM, ARCHER?" DEREK asked when we were in Almay's bedchamber at our club. I doctored the cut on Almay's arm, thankful the knife blade hadn't severed anything vital. I washed and bandaged the wound, hoping it didn't take sick.

"Say?" I asked distractedly.

"He means what did you do to make Perkins finally confess?" Almay said irritably. Pain made him tetchy. "Or had drawing blood from me cooled his defiance?"

I couldn't explain about my night-slayer, so I shrugged and rolled up the extra bandage I hadn't used. "Oh, I threatened him with this and that."

"Archer has were-beasts turning to him for help," Derek said. "Perhaps he suggested how displeased they'd be if Perkins didn't own up. One of them is a pack guard, he said? Whatever that is."

"A man with a wolf's eyes and a bad temper." I hadn't known Seamus's title, but it fit him. "It would not do well to make one angry."

Derek looked me up and down. "I will do my best not to make *you* angry either."

"You are safe, Chase." I chuckled but neither Chase nor Almay appeared to be reassured.

"Good thing the Runner was there," Almay remarked. "Your doing, Archer?"

"Not me," I said. "Never saw the man."

"Mine," Derek said calmly. "Hawthorne is an old friend. Long story," he added as both Almay and I stared at him. "I asked him to come with me and to linger discreetly. I had a feeling Archer brought us there for a reason."

"I'd have invited a Runner if I'd thought of it," I said. "Though I'd worry that Perkins would know him. Runners do give evidence at the Old Bailey. Their paths might have crossed before."

"Which is why I asked Hawthorne to be discreet. He stayed out of Perkins's line of sight but listened to every word."

"I thank you, then," I said in sincerity. "A timely aid."

"Not at all." Derek gave me a modest nod. "You're an old friend, Archer. Always happy to help."

"As am I," Almay put in. "But not with my blood next time, if you please."

"Do not be so quick to chase a villain, then," I admonished.

Derek curtailed Almay's annoyed reply by reaching for a cut-glass decanter on the nearby table.

"Brandy, gentlemen?" he asked.

"Yes, indeed," I said, and Almay nodded. "I believe inebriation is in order."

"I wholeheartedly concur," Derek said. He poured brandy into the glasses, and we fell to it.

CHAPTER EIGHT

I did not see Kieran until a few days later. As I walked home from an obligatory and uncomfortable visit with my brother in Berkeley Square in the late afternoon, a dark coach pulled up beside me and its door opened.

I looked up to see Kieran inside, with Seamus opposite him.

"Get in," Seamus commanded me.

I did not want to sit next to Seamus as I'd done for my first ride in this carriage, but I didn't think he'd let me plop myself beside Kieran. Seamus solved the dilemma by moving across to Kieran's side, leaving the opposite seat empty.

I settled myself in, deciding to enjoy the comfort of Kieran's luxurious carriage, no matter what my danger.

"You have done us a good turn," Kieran said without bothering with greetings or inquiries about my health. "I have told others you are a friend to the weres."

"Means we can't kill you when we see you coming," Seamus clarified. He sounded disappointed.

"And my pack owes you a favor," Kieran continued, ignoring Seamus. "Make certain it is a worthwhile one."

In other words, I wasn't to waste their time. Seamus didn't have to translate that for me.

"Perkins will stand in the Old Bailey soon," I said, relating what a grim-faced Almay had told me this morning. "Not in the position he usually does," I added with a touch of dark humor. "Copeland's sister and husband are prosecuting him for the death their brother."

Kieran listened to me patiently, but it was obvious he had no interest in the details. "You are an uncommon man, Mr. Archer."

"So my brother tells me," I said lightly. "As you have found out all about him, you'll know what an ass he is, so it might not be a compliment."

"Take it as one," Kieran advised. "You trusted us when everything about your world told you not to, unusual in a human. I'd like to claim were-beasts never seek convenient answers, but that would not be true. We are as fallible as you, in certain circumstances."

I wasn't certain how to respond, so I said nothing. Seamus's expression of disgust told me he did not agree with Kieran's assessment.

I wondered at the connection between them, and whether Seamus served Kieran reluctantly or with great loyalty. As I planned never to seek them out again, I possibly would not discover the answer.

"This is Tottenham Court Road," I said as the carriage turned a corner and the conversation seemed to have ended. "You can let me down here."

"Afraid to be seen with weres?" Seamus sneered.

"I was thinking you might not want to be seen in Gower Street. Or anywhere close to where your half-human friend dwells."

Seamus's growls filled the coach. Kieran lifted a hand to quiet him, but the eyes he turned on me were wolf-hard.

"You will stay away from Queen Anne Street," he stated. "Not even to pass through. Go around, and quell your curiosity about the half-were. He is not a pleasant soul, and seeking him out could mean your death."

I believed him. "I have plenty of dangerous enemies already, I assure you. I will keep my distance."

Kieran nodded as though we'd made a pact. Seamus still watched me, but I didn't expect him to trust me. As long as Seamus remained in Whitechapel and far from me, however, I'd be content.

The coach pulled into a small lane that led to Bedford Square and halted at Kieran's command. There was just enough room to open the door, and I squeezed myself out and stepped against a wall so the wheels would not crush me when the carriage moved on.

Kieran leaned out the window. "Thank you, Mr. Archer. You have earned my regard."

He announced this as though he said it to very few, so I tipped my hat and bowed to him, as much as the narrow space allowed. "I am honored, Mr. Hacault."

Kieran returned the bow then withdrew. The coach started, taking them on toward Bedford Square. The carriage turned the corner and was lost to sight.

A man had emerged from a house opposite and stood staring at me. Though Bedford Square boasted large and lush homes, the inhabitants probably did not halt their coaches in this tiny lane to disgorge passengers, and those conveyances did not contain weres.

I nodded to him and trudged on toward the square, darkening skies and flakes of falling snow encouraging me to get indoors.

———

I spent the evening dining with fellow members of my club then decided to turn in early. This afternoon's encounter with Kieran had unsettled me.

Though I was glad he'd showed gratitude for my help, I wished that the entire incident, from my walk home on New Year's Eve to Kieran's dismissal this afternoon, had never happened.

But it had. I'd learned that were-beasts could be more honorable than human beings in positions of trust, and that my faith in the law and its traders was misplaced.

I'd also learned firsthand how dangerous were-beasts could be, recalling Seamus's determination to kill me in two instances. I'd looked into his eyes and seen my own death.

Perkins must have done the same when my lady night-slayer caught him. I had to feel sorry for the poor bastard.

Once in my room, I dropped into the chair by the fire, toed off my uncomfortable boots, and stretched my stockinged feet toward the flames. I heaved a sigh, closing my eyes.

"Champagne?"

I jumped awake to find my lady night-slayer standing over me with a bottle in her hand.

I rubbed my eyes and tried to clear my head. She looked different tonight, and it took me a moment to realize she'd eschewed her modest garb of dark frocks and bonnets for a white and gold tissue creation that slid down her shoulders. Her hair was dressed in a knot with cascading ringlets, and diamonds encircled her neck.

She resembled the ladies at the New Year's ball I'd attended, except that her eyes were darker than night, and she didn't look through me in search of someone more interesting.

I gripped the arms of my chair. "Do you drink champagne?"

She smiled. "I imbibe many things."

Before I could think of a reply, she reached over and unwound the loosened cravat from my neck. As I sat still, throat tight, she wrapped the cravat over the top of the champagne bottle and began to work out the cork.

"You know, Napoleon's officers opened those with their sabers," I babbled. "One stroke, and they were done. They packed bottles of champagne at Waterloo to celebrate their inevitable victory. We found so many on the fields …"

I trailed off, not wanting to remember the carnage and the groans of the dying, our mixture of triumph and relief that the emperor had been vanquished at last.

The bottle opened with a muffled *bang* that made me jump. My night-slayer poured the frothing liquid into two glasses on my side table. The glasses weren't mine, so she must have brought them with her as well.

She set down the bottle and handed me a goblet. "You were not able to properly celebrate the New Year. Werebeasts and murder can be most distracting."

"You are in a puckish mood this evening," I said as I took the offered glass.

"I saw my daughter today. From afar, of course." I sensed both the sadness and the joy that encounter had brought. "Because of you, I *can* see her. She has grown to be so beautiful ..."

I raised my glass, hoping to ease her pain. "To Anne," I said. "The loveliest of ladies."

Her smile turned wistful. "To my Anne."

We drank. She swallowed without choking or spitting out the liquid as though her body rejected anything but blood. Another myth quelled.

"To you," I said, saluting her. "For rushing to my side and saving my life. Yet again."

"And to you, Robert Archer," she countered. "Happy New Year."

She leaned closer, putting her lips near my bare throat, her breath chilling instead of warming. My skin prickled, and I stifled a gasp.

She backed away, her wide smile telling me she enjoyed disconcerting me.

We drank again, her dark eyes pinning me but not revealing what was behind the mystery inside them.

"Happy New Year," I told her.

For answer, she laughed. She tossed back the contents of her glass, brushed fingers over my exposed neck, and suddenly was gone. The draft of her passing froze me, and I was left alone and shivering.

At least, I reflected as I reached for the bottle beside me, she'd left the champagne.

What did it say about my life that the only woman in it was terrifying?

"Happy New Year," I whispered to the air, and then quiet settled, mercifully, on me once more.

AUTHOR'S NOTE

Thank you for reading!

As Ashley Gardner, I don't as a rule write paranormal or supernatural mysteries, but the voice and flavor of this one is closer to my Ashley Gardner books, so I chose that pen name for it. I wrote this story before I began the Captain Lacey Regency Mysteries, and you might see some parallels between Captain Lacey and Robert Archer, though I think Lacey has a little more determination to resolve problems on his own, plus wouldn't dream of breaking anyone's marital vows.

A Matter of Honor came out of the phase of my writing when I planned to be a fantasy author, but my career went a very different direction, to my surprise. However, I enjoy dabbling in fantasy / paranormal (as evidenced by my long-running paranormal romance series and the contemporary fantasy I write as Allyson James).

If you are interested in more conventional historical mysteries, see the Captain Lacey Regency Mysteries, the Leonidas the Gladiator Mysteries, and the Below Stairs

Mysteries (which I write as Jennifer Ashley). For fantasy, see the Stormwalker series I write as Allyson James (contemporary-set stories in the Southwestern U.S.).

I hope you enjoyed this story, a taste of the supernatural side of my imagination.

There will be more Robert Archer paranormal historical mysteries in the future.

All my best,

Ashley Gardner

HISTORICAL MYSTERIES BY ASHLEY GARDNER

Robert Archer Paranormal Mysteries

A Matter of Honor

A Matter at New Year's

Leonidas the Gladiator Mysteries

Blood of a Gladiator

Blood Debts

A Gladiator's Tale

A Gladiator's Tale

The Ring that Caesar Wore

Brother at Arms

Captain Lacey Regency Mystery Series

The Hanover Square Affair

A Regimental Murder

The Glass House

The Sudbury School Murders

The Necklace Affair

A Body in Berkeley Square

A Covent Garden Mystery

A Death in Norfolk

A Disappearance in Drury Lane

Murder in Grosvenor Square

The Thames River Murders

The Alexandria Affair

A Mystery at Carlton House

Murder in St. Giles

Death at Brighton Pavilion

The Custom House Murders

Murder in the Eternal City

A Darkness in Seven Dials

The Gentleman's Walking Stick

(short stories: in print in

The Necklace Affair and Other Stories)

Kat Holloway "Below Stairs" Victorian Mysteries

(writing as Jennifer Ashley)

A Soupçon of Poison

Death Below Stairs

Scandal Above Stairs

Death in Kew Gardens

Murder in the East End

Death at the Crystal Palace

The Secret of Bow Lane

The Price of Lemon Cake

(novella)

Mrs. Holloway's Christmas Pudding

(holiday novella)

Speculations in Sin

A Measure of Menace

(novella)

A Moveable Feast

(novella)

A Silence in Belgrave Square

Mystery Anthologies

Past Crimes

ABOUT THE AUTHOR

USA Today Bestselling author Ashley Gardner is a pseudonym for *New York Times* bestselling author Jennifer Ashley. Under both names—and a third, Allyson James—Ashley has written more than 100 published novels and novellas in mystery, romance, fantasy, and historical fiction. Ashley's books have been translated into more than a dozen different languages and have earned starred reviews in *Publisher's Weekly* and *Booklist*. When she isn't writing, she indulges her love for history by researching and building miniature houses and furniture from many periods, and playing classical guitar and piano.

More about the Captain Lacey series can be found at the website: www.gardnermysteries.com. Stay up to date on new releases by joining her email alerts here: http://eepurl.com/5n7rz

Follow Ashley Gardner
www.gardnermysteries.com

www.ingramcontent.com/pod-product-compliance
Lightning Source LLC
Chambersburg PA
CBHW031624310726
48974CB00003B/813